Who Stole Stacey Orpington's Tiara?

LOLA SMITH: The attractive stewardess had been carrying a hatbox identical to Stacey's. Perhaps it was all an innocent mistake—but there was nothing innocent about Lola's death.

BARBARA DONALDSON: On her way to Abu Dhabi, the oil baron's wife had flashed some jewelry of her own. No sooner had Stacey absolved her of the crime, when she dropped out of sight.

EUSTACE ORPINGTON-BLAINE: Stacey's aristocratic cousin picked a bad time to show up out of the blue. Then, after whisking her off to his country home, he picked an even worse time to disappear...

IMELDA BUTLER: The cover girl promised to use her contacts to help get Stacey's jewelry back. Stacey wanted to trust the beautiful creature, but somehow, something kept getting in the way...

"THE TWO MEN": Handcuffed together in First Class, they were immediately recognizable as a policeman and his prisoner. But which was which, and where did they go after they got off the plane?

MARIAN BABSON

BEJEWELLED DEATH

A MYSTERY

WARNER BOOKS

A Time Warner Company

All the characters and events portrayed in this story are fictitious.

WARNER BOOKS EDITION

This Warner Books Edition is published by arrangement with Walker and Company.

Cover illustration by Phillip Singer
Cover design by Jackie Merri Meyer

Warner Books, Inc.
666 Fifth Avenue
New York, N.Y. 10103

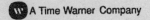 A Time Warner Company

Printed in the United States of America

First Warner Books Printing: April, 1991

10 9 8 7 6 5 4 3 2

CHAPTER 1

A SINGLE LIGHT BEAMED OUT FROM THE SECOND-FLOOR corner window of the Orpington Memorial Museum. The pale glow fell upon the smooth green lawn surrounding the white clapboard house but did not quite reach the answering glow from the street lamp on the corner. Nothing moved in the dark green shadowed sweep between the brighter areas.

Hardly surprising, of course, at that hour of the night. Thringsby, Massachusetts, was something short of a bustling metropolis even during the height of its morning and evening rush hours.

Inside the lighted room, the loudest sound was the irritating buzz of a mosquito circling around the man and woman standing by the display case in the center of the room. Only an occasional brushing motion of her hand betrayed that the woman was aware of the mosquito at all. The man bending over the display case was so totally

1

absorbed in what he was doing that he seemed to forget for minutes at a time that the woman was in the room with him; he had not even noticed the mosquito. His hands were trembling as he fumbled for the release catch on the display case.

"You've turned off the burglar alarm?" She could not help asking, even though she knew it would annoy him.

"Or course I've turned off the burglar alarm." He raised his head to glare at her. "Do you imagine I'd forget a thing like that? We don't want the police rushing in here to discover what we're doing. You know there isn't one of them who can keep his mouth shut."

"They are a bit fond of gossip," she admitted. "You can't blame them. It would be a change from motoring offenses, drunks and stray cows wandering on to the public highway."

He returned to his task without deigning to answer. He released the catch and raised the glass lid.

Stacey caught the card on top as it started to slide off to the floor. It would be placed inside the case when they had finished. In neat black lettering, it informed any interested member of the public:

THIS EXHIBIT HAS BEEN TEMPORARILY
REMOVED FOR CLEANING.

If they believed that, they'd believe anything. There were times when Gordon carried his passion for security to ridiculous extremes.

"Aaahh . . ." Delicately he lifted the priceless tiara from the black velvet mound. Pinwheels of reflected brilliance danced across the room as the light caught and struck fire from the diamonds.

He stooped and transferred it swiftly to a similar mound, custom-built within the deceptively ordinary carrying case. Well, almost ordinary.

Stacey surveyed it with dissatisfaction.

"I wish you'd remember to pull down the shade." Straightening, Gordon glanced at the window with equal dissatisfaction. "Do it now... if you please."

"We're on the second floor, for heaven's sake!" Extremes again. But she crossed to the window and lowered the shade. It was wiser to humor him when he was in this mood, although she could not keep from registering her protest. "Who do you imagine might be looking in at us?"

"You never can tell," he said portentously. "You can see a lot through a lighted window if you're viewing from a distance."

"They'd have to have binoculars!"

"Precisely." He nodded. "We can't be too careful. Given the circumstances."

The circumstances. Stacey watched in silence as he carefully transferred the remainder of the jewels into the neat little pockets sewn along the side of the case. Small velvet flaps folded over to conceal the glittering contents once they had been placed in the pockets. Mrs. Thringsby was an obsessive needle-woman and had obviously enjoyed herself hugely fashioning the elaborate aids to deception.

"Your mother did a marvelous job," she said as Gordon doubled the jewelled choker and stowed it away in the larger pocket prepared for it. A place for everything and everything in its place—just like the Thringsby house.

"She did, didn't she?" He folded down the flap and gave it a self-satisfied little pat, taking part of the credit for himself. "Of course, it was quite tricky gluing it in over the existing lining. I thought I'd never get it smoothed into place before the glue dried. But you can see, it works quite well. No one would ever guess what you were carrying."

Simultaneously, their eyes fell on the tiara clamped into the center of the case. A double tiara, actually, which could be taken apart and used as two different tiaras or, as now, cleverly fitted together to make one impressive—and quite heavy—tiara. The conventional diamond tiara interlaced with the gemstone tiara of rubies, sapphires, emeralds and fire opals set in unswept curves to give an effect of a halo of flames dancing around the head of the wearer. Fabulously valuable in itself, as a work of art it was unique and priceless. Particularly when taken together with the rest of the set which, in the Victorian way, had been relentlessly matched and intended to adorn every portion of the body which could be decently displayed. There were earrings, bracelets, choker, long necklace with detachable brooch, several other brooches designed to be worn in their own right, plus a posy-holder. There was even—naughtily—a jewelled garter which it was somehow impossible to imagine Great Grand-Aunt Eustacia ever wearing, not even as a private joke in the earliest days of marriage.

"You can just drop some scarves and perhaps a blouse over that—" Gordon was still frowning thoughtfully at the tiara. "It's clamped into place, so it won't move when you're carrying the case. Nothing will move or rattle. It should be perfectly safe. No one would ever guess you were carrying a king's ransom in there."

"I hope not," Stacey said uneasily. "I just wish you could have found a different sort of case."

"And what is wrong with this one?" Gordon asked coldly. "It suits the purpose perfectly."

"It's a hat-box," Stacey complained. "No one has carried a hat-box since *Night Must Fall* gave them such a bad name."

"That's ridiculous, Stacey," he said huffily. "Lots of people carry hat-boxes."

"When did you last see anyone carrying a hat-box?"

"The day I bought this," he said triumphantly. "They were selling like hot cakes. Practically everyone in Filene's Basement that day was buying one."

"Perhaps they're having a revival." She shrugged, but he frowned, reminded of an old grievance. He had never really approved of her long and enthusiastic involvement with the Thringsby Players. Still less after last winter's presentation of *The Desert Song* when he had protested her (admittedly) skimpy costume of chiffon and rhinestones.

("Don't be silly. It's a lot more than I wear at the beach in the summer." ... "At the beach, you are not standing in the dark with a spotlight on you!")

"Stacey—" His voice was solemn, he had obviously decided to ignore the opening that could lead back into an old familiar argument in favor of the current problem. "Stacey, are you sure you don't mind?"

"Mind?" For a moment, he had lost her. "I'm really looking forward to the trip. I've always wanted to see England. And everything ought to be all right. The odds against anything happening are roughly the same as the odds that the plane might crash. In which case," she added with a trace of bitterness, "the jewels will come through the wreck in a lot better condition than I will."

"That's what I mean." He had caught the note of bitterness. "The jewels..." He snapped down the lid of the hat-box, not meeting her eyes. "Doesn't it ever bother you...the thought that they ought to be yours? Would have been yours, if only...?"

"If only Great-Grand-Aunt Eustacia had been less of a raving egomaniac?" She finished the thought for him, more brutally than he would have done. Of course, as Curator of the Orpington Memorial Museum, he would be unwilling to malign his benefactress. Unwilling—or afraid to. Anyone who had ever known Great-Grand-Aunt Eustacia, particularly in the closing years of her inordinately long life, would always harbor a slight doubt that even six feet of earth could keep her from finding some way to answer back.

"Well..." Involuntarily he glanced over his shoulder. "If she hadn't wanted to perpetuate the Orpington name—which was her married name, in any case...And she made the rest of her family—your family—change to the Orpington name by deed poll...And, after all that...in the end..." With an apologetic smile, he let the thought trail off. It was the closest he had ever come to discussing the situation; it was probably as close as he ever would come. Frank and full discussions were not Gordon's line of country. He excelled in conciliation, mediation...

"*Dithering*," Great-Grand-Aunt Eustacia would have said.

Nevertheless, he was a Thringsby. The Thringsbys had founded the town to which they had given their name. It was hardly their fault that, due to the geographical location, Thringsby never evolved into the thriving city they had envisaged. In New England, the seacoast towns had become the primary centers of commerce, with those built on rivers in secondary positions. A landlocked town was foredoomed to be of lesser importance, however beloved by certain of its citizens, beyond mere loyalty, almost to the point of irrationality.

As witness Great-Grand-Aunt Eustacia, whose ancestors had had the bad judgement to arrive in Thringsby a quarter of a century later than the founding family and discovered that all the relevant place names had been pre-empted. A failing she had never forgiven them—and which possibly explained her devotion to the Orpington name and title. What with Thringsby itself, Thringsby Lake, Thringsby Landing, Thringsby Park and Thringsby Crossing, there was little place for any other family to leave its mark.

But Great-Grand-Aunt Eustacia had finally found a way. The promised bequest of the Orpington regalia had been too much to resist and the Thringsby Museum had become the Orpington Memorial Museum, with the Orpington treasure on show on permanent loan during Great-Grand-Aunt Eustacia's lifetime and a permanent acquisition upon her death—on condition that the name of the museum never be changed again. It was a small price for the citizens of Thringsby to pay for a treasure they could never have afforded to buy.

Buy? They couldn't even afford the insurance premi-

ums on it. The Orpington Memorial Museum was no
alone in this. Small local museums all over the worle
were hugging their treasures to their bosoms, keeping a
low profile and hoping that nobody would notice that a
small fortune was tucked away in a building that could be
broken into by any reasonably bright five-year-old wielding
one of Granny's discarded hairpins.

"It might all have been yours, Stacey. If only . . . things
had been different." Again he glanced guiltily over his
shoulder. "Doesn't the thought ever . . . bother you?"

"Not inordinately," she answered truthfully. "Where
could I ever wear such things in this country? I doubt if
there are many occasions where they could be worn
even in England, these days."

"That's beside the point and you know it. I mean, the
pieces could have been sold. Separately, if necessary. Or
perhaps broken up and the gems taken out of their settings
and sold. That way, you still could have retained some of
the pieces that could be worn today, like the earrings and
bracelets, and have lived luxuriously on the rest."

"Gordon! Great-Grand-Aunt Eustacia would come back
and haunt you to the end of your days if she could hear
you say a thing like that! Besides, you know the set
wouldn't be half so valuable broken up."

Even less so, if the gems were removed from their
settings. The elaborate suite was the creation of the
legendary jeweller, Duvanov, who had served his appren-
ticeship in the Fabergé workshop before moving to England
to set up his own business and become one of the most
brilliant and fashionable jewellers of a brilliant and fashionable age.

The Orpington Suite had been specially designed to celebrate the marriage of Great-Grand-Aunt Eustacia to the Earl of Orpington and was, she always claimed, his wedding present to her. It was unfortunate that the Orpington family had been under the impression that the jewels were to become part of the family heritage, as they undoubtedly would have been had the marriage lasted.

Unfortunately, it hadn't and Great-Grand-Aunt Eustacia had gathered up her skirts and what she considered her rightful spoils and retreated to her native land, pursued by threats of legal action which never materialized. Unpleasant rumors had abounded, whispers that there had been another little bundle which she really ought to have brought home with her, but Great-Grand-Aunt Eustacia had remained undisturbed by them.

(*"I never did anything to be ashamed of,"* she had once said in a rare moment of self-justification at a family gathering. *"And—"* she had run her fingers lovingly over the jewelled choker—*"I left behind nothing of any value."*)

Those who knew her whispered that she would have considered a female child of no value since, under the English law of male primogeniture, only a male heir could succeed to the title and estate. There were further suggestions that she had departed because she was unable to have another child and did not wish to watch her husband perhaps turn to another woman to ensure succession.

In the event, the Earl of Orpington had a nasty accident in the hunting field and the subsequent loss of the title and devolvement of the estate upon a remote male cousin had left Great-Grand-Aunt Eustacia in undisputed possession of her loot.

"Just the same, Stacey. I've wondered sometimes if..." Gordon did not quite meet her eyes. "If you haven't been conscious of a certain... injustice..."

"Gordon!" An inkling of what he was driving at brought her head up sharply and narrowed her eyes. "If you'd rather not *trust* me with the Orpington Bequest, we can forget the whole thing here and now!"

"That isn't what I meant," he said unhappily, every crease in his forehead proclaiming that it was. "I just thought..." He glanced over his shoulder toward the wall from which the full-length portrait of Great-Grand-Aunt Eustacia in full regalia painted by John Singer Sargent dominated the room.

"I don't know what I mean," he admitted limply. "The arrangements have all been made and we're committed to this course of action. I just wish..." He let the thought trail off. Perhaps he did not know what he wished himself.

"Opening night nerves," Stacey diagnosed crisply. "You're thinking of all the things that might go wrong. It's highly unlikely that anything will. People are doing this all the time, all over the world."

"I know," he said. "And it doesn't say much for the state of the world that respectable institutions should be reduced to this sort of behavior."

They both surveyed the hat-box with dissatisfaction.

He was right, of course. It was ludicrous that reputable curators of museums, art galleries, libraries and private collections should be forced into the sort of cloak-and-dagger antics that used to be associated with spies and French farces.

But it was the way of the world these days. Museums which were unable to afford the insurance premiums for treasures safely held behind locked doors and guarded by alarm systems were still less able to pay the whacking premiums for transit insurance when these artifacts were being moved from place to place or sent out on loan to exhibitions. It was cheaper and, in most cases, just as safe to send them by a courier travelling first class who could carry them, if they were small enough, or allow them out of sight only for the minimum length of time if their size made it necessary for them to travel in the cargo hold.

The Orpington Bequest fitted neatly into the hat-box and was not so heavy that it could not be carried with moderate ease. (Although there must have been moments toward the end of a long evening when Great-Grand-Aunt Eustacia, wearing the full suite, must have swayed like a sapling in a gale.)

"Really—" Gordon seemed to be trying to cheer himself as much as her—"it will be out of your hands in twenty-four hours. Until the return trip, that is. And I'll be with you then."

"Yes," she said.

"You can put it in the hotel safe as soon as you arrive and contact the exhibition organizers. Then they can either come over and collect it, or you can deliver it to the Duvanov Exhibition yourself and it will be their responsibility. I understand," he added wistfully, "that *they'll* have full insurance cover for the duration of the exhibition."

"They probably get preferential short-term rates from Lloyds of London," she agreed. It was silly to be nervous. As Gordon had pointed out, the responsibility would be hers only for about twenty-four hours. It was her first trip to Europe and it was being paid for by the Duvanov Exhibition which wanted to mount the Orpington Bequest as the showpiece of the exhibition, since it was the last of the monumental suites created by Duvanov himself to have survived—still intact—wars, revolutions and the vicissitudes of the years.

She would travel first class all the way and once she had handed over the hat-box, her time was her own to explore and enjoy a tourist's life. All she had to do was be the courier and guardian while the Orpington Bequest was in transit. It was cheap at the price.

"Well." Gordon picked up the hat-box; he would not deliver it into her care until next day. "There's nothing else to be done here. I'll collect you and drive you to the airport in the morning."

"Fine." she sighed faintly.

"You needn't let it worry you, Stacey. You won't be at all conspicuous. I'm sure there'll be plenty of people travelling with hat-boxes."

CHAPTER 2

At first glance, it seemed that Gordon was right. The hat-box was "in" again. Either that, or Filene's price had been so low as to be irresistible to more than Gordon. They were hardly through the doors at Logan Airport when she could see at least three hat-boxes identical to the one she would carry.

"You check your luggage through." He deposited her at the end of a long line winding across the lobby. "I'll hold on to the hat-box for you." He smiled conspiratorially. "We wouldn't want anyone to take that away from you and send it off with the rest of your bags. That's going to be your cabin baggage."

"Why don't you get me a couple of magazines for the flight?" she suggested, juggling handbag, tickets and passport and trying to resist the temptation to open her handbag again and make sure her travellers checks were still there. Gordon's anxiety was infecting her. Futhermore, if he didn't stop making fatuous remarks in a voice charged with meaning, people around them might begin to put two and two together. She had not Gordon's infinite disdain for the mental ability of the ordinary citizen. Perhaps because she realized that, however unexceptional they appeared, few people were really ordinary.

"Yes. Fine." All but hugging the hat-box to him, he glanced around suspiciously. There were three similar hat-boxes ahead of them in the queue. One was just being edged along with the rest of her luggage by the matron now coming to the head of the line; another was carried casually by a vaguely familiar-looking young woman with a rather-too-flawless makeup; the third was deposited incongruously at the feet of a wiry young man of medium height who looked both haggard and determined. At the moment, he had his eyes closed against the overhead neon lights. Too much of a going-away party last night, perhaps.

"I *told* you hat-boxes were popular," Gordon said, as an air hostess walked past carrying another one.

"They must have been the bargain of the year," Stacey agreed. The line moved forward again; it was moving more quickly than she had dared hope.

"I'll get your magazines." Gordon measured the length of the queue. "I'll be right back. Anything special you want?"

"Just a good selection," Stacey called after him as he moved away without waiting for an answer.

Other people were joining the line behind her. She became aware of them when she was suddenly, roughly, jostled.

"Excuse me," the man said. "I was pushed. I didn't mean to bump into you. I hope you're all right."

"Quite all right." Stacey turned, smiling automatically. "It is pretty crowded here."

"We aren't all bound for the same destinations," he assured her comfortingly. "Paris . . . London . . . Athens . . . Rome . . . we're all in the same line until they separate the sheep from the goats . . ." He paused hopefully. "I'm bound for London myself. Flight 1302."

"So am I." There was no point in being coy, they'd meet aboard the flight, in which case it would be more embarrassing to have tried to deny it than to admit him as a fellow passenger.

"Well, great!" He greeted the news joyously, then seemed to have second thoughts. "Er . . . I'm afraid I'm a first-class passenger. The University is paying. But perhaps we can meet for a drink in the cocktail lounge—?"

"I'm first-class myself." She raised her own colors. "The museum is paying . . ."

"Well, great!" He beamed down at her. "I'm George Cabot, Professor Cabot. We obviously have a lot in common. The expense account intelligentsia—it makes a change from your usual account executives and managing directors."

There was a sudden undignified scramble as everyone grabbed for their luggage and the line advanced several paces.

The man ahead of them, who had been forced to open his eyes as a result of the activity, now looked around uneasily as though searching for someone. Then his eyes closed again and he seemed to sink back into his doze.

Still more would-be passengers had assembled behind them, surrounded by friends and families come to see them off. It was the usual unsatisfactory crowd scene, fraught with emotion and fraying tempers. Stacey's spirit was buoyed up by the realization that this time it was she who was about to board a plane and be lifted out of it all.

In the distance, a child started to cry fretfully. In automatic response, the man ahead lurched out of line and had gone several steps before his eyes opened. He looked around, pinpointed the source of the tears as a toddler clinging to the jeans of its exasperated mother and, with an apologetic grimace to no one in particular, he resumed his place. This time, however, he kept his eyes open and seemed to be searching for someone. His wife and child, perhaps, Stacey thought, adding up the clues in the way that one does when observing the behavior of strangers.

"Here we are." Gordon appeared beside her, reclaiming her attention. "And look—" He nodded toward the tall, exquisite beauty now standing at the check-in desk, then ruffled through the pile of magazines. "She's on the cover of *Vogue* this month. I thought she looked familiar. Do you suppose she's on your flight?"

"Possibly." Stacey was aware that Professor Cabot was straining forward, obviously yearning to join in the conversation. At the same time, she was preternaturally conscious of the shiny black hat-box over Gordon's arm, twin to the hat-box the model was carrying. Soon now, Gordon was going to transfer the hat-box into her sole care and she would be responsible for an irreplaceable artistic treasure worth a fortune.

Stacey shifted her position slightly so that the man behind could have no casual opportunity to slide into the conversation. Suddenly she felt like a child again, with the age-old warning ringing in her ears: *Don't speak to strangers*. It was particularly good advice to the guardian of an uninsured jewellery collection.

This must be the way heiresses felt. Always a little bit on guard. Always wondering whether the man was as pleasant and friendly as he seemed or whether he was a fortune-hunter wearing a mask as he stalked the woman's bank account rather than the woman herself.

If things had been different, it might have been a way of life for her. If Great-Grand-Aunt Eustacia had kept the jewels and allowed them to be handed down in the family rather than bestowing them on a museum...

But no one could possibly know what she was carrying. Certainly no one would ever suspect that an ordinary hat-box, similar to dozens of others, without even a special lock, could contain anything worth stealing. Not without inside information.

Suddenly, the elaborate precautions Gordon had taken to keep news of the museum loan-out from the citizens of Thringsby no longer seemed amusing, but good sound common sense.

The line inched along, to the increasing agitation of another possessor of a shiny black hat-box. He seemed to be measuring the distance left between himself and the check-in desk, possibly with a view to asking someone else in the line to keep his place while he carried out an urgent errand.

Just as he seemed about to do so, a small girl with dark hair and dark intense eyes materialized at his side. She was perhaps seven or eight and carrying a pile of comic books. Ignoring the man, she took possession of the hat-box, opened it and placed the comic books inside on top of what appeared to be a heap of dolls. The man relaxed somewhat, but still seemed to be looking for someone else.

The line moved forward again. Gordon shifted the hat-box on his arm. "Nearly time," he said.

"Yes." She checked her watch, already longing for the moment when she would pass into the departure lounge and leave him behind. They had said everything there was to say, they could not discuss the matter most urgently on their minds. It was time to say goodbye.

But they were trapped in this endless line.

"Hor! Hey, Hor!" The shout cut across all thought and caught everyone's attention. Some people smiled, some frowned. The boy racing across the lobby was oblivious of them all. "Hor!" he cried again, sliding to a stop beside the small thin girl, who looked at him with disfavor.

"Marvin." The man winced and spoke coldly and clearly. "I have told you before. Hor is not the diminutive of Hortense!"

"Why not?" the boy asked carefully. He was about eleven or twelve and there seemed a faint raffishness about him which augured ill for his future. "I mean, if Marv is short for Marvin, and Al is short for Alistair—"

"Al is not short for Alistair." The man spoke through clenched teeth. "I have never been called Al in my life."

"Alis?" He was willing to be corrected.

"My name is Alistair," the man said firmly. "My friends call me Alistair. You, however, may call me Mr. Lord."

"You're mad at me again. I can tell—" Marvin

shrugged his shoulders, thereby calling attention to the fact that they were decorated by a strange pattern of loose-hanging threads. He wore a vaguely military style jacket, the sleeves of which also displayed loose threads around chevron-shaped slightly darker patches. The whole gave rise to a vision of epaulettes having been ripped off and stripes torn away.

"Hor-*tense*—" He turned with elaborate patience to the girl. "Hor-tense, come and see—"

"Oh no you don't!" The man's hand clamped down on his shoulder. "You're both staying right here. We're almost at the check-in desk."

"But it will only take a minute—" Marvin wriggled experimentally, but the hand did not release its hold.

"Okay," he capitulated. "But it's your fault that Hortense misses out—"

The little girl gave a peculiarly Gallic shrug, quite unlike Marvin's earlier shrug. "*N'importe*," she said. So she was French.

Marvin was definitely American, and the man's accent, although predominantly mid-Atlantic, slipped over into English-English under stress.

An odd collection. Where was the woman who would presumably unite them and explain their having come together? Stacey glanced around, but Alistair Lord no longer was searching for anyone else. His party, it seemed, was complete; his relief was evident, for the next shift forward would bring them up to the check-in desk. They had reassembled just in time.

"Well, nearly there." Gordon tightened his grip on the hat-box as though reluctant to relinquish it. "I'll follow you over in just two more weeks. We can do some sightseeing together before we come home again."

"Fine." It was hard to summon up that first fine enthusiasm when the same information was being imparted for the umpteenth time.

The man and the children picked up their hand luggage and headed for the security check. The line shuffled forward again.

"Well . . ." He moved along beside her. She wondered if he would be able to bring himself to part with the hat-box. Gordon always had difficulty delegating authority. That was his trouble—among others.

But this was neither the time nor the place to go into deep contemplation of Gordon's shortcomings. Nor the fact that, because they both worked for the museum and were thereby considered to be on an intellectual plane, Thringsby had inevitably paired them off until they now had what used to be known as an "understanding." She had been promising herself for some time that she was going to sit down quietly to think the situation through some day and come to some conclusion about it before it was too late.

Somehow the opportunity had not yet come; the necessary length of uninterrupted time had never materialized. Perhaps, on this trip . . .

Abruptly, they were at the check-in desk; there was the flurry of activity; time telescoped in its capricious way and they were at the entrance to the security arch, finally saying goodbye.

"I'll see you in two weeks—that isn't long." Still clutching the hat-box, Gordon aimed a peck at her cheek.

"Goodbye, Gordon." Taking a firm grip on the carrying strap, she wrested the hat-box from him.

"It won't be long," he said, as she turned away.

Ahead of her, the metal detector abruptly buzzed its grim warning, bringing everything to a standstill. The guard had been passing the wand over the child's hat-box. He stared incredulously at the little girl, then raised his eyes to the man accompanying her.

"All right," he said. "Open it and let's see what's inside."

"*Oui*," Hortense said happily. Ceremoniously, she unlocked the hat-box and lifted out the doll on top. "This is Suzette," she introduced. "And Pierrot—" It was a painted tumbler toy, an acrobat in a walking frame. She set it on the counter beside Suzette. "And Snoopy—" She took out the ubiquitous overstuffed dog with long floppy black ears. Beneath it was a jumble of comic books and lesser toys which the guard sorted through.

"Here we are." He picked up a large tin paintbox. "This is probably—"

The painted Pierrot had been rocking gently in his frame, now, its delicate balance set in motion, the Pierrot made a long lazy somersault over the balance bar of his frame which, in turn, rocked the frame forward, providing enough impulse to send the doll into another somersault. At which, the whole action repeated itself and the doll rocked and somersaulted in slow progress across the counter, a miniature perpetual motion machine.

"Bad Pierrot!" Hortense caught it just before it tumbled to the floor. "Stay still."

"That's it." The guard grinned. "The thing is weighted, probably with lead. Between that and the paintbox, it's no wonder the buzzer sounded."

The atmosphere lightened perceptibly. The guard helped Hortense repack her hat-box and waved them through.

Stacey did not breathe her own sigh of relief until she was safely past the security station, but it appeared that the metal detector only detected base metals and not precious ones. She passed without incident.

CHAPTER 3

ONCE EVERYONE HAD BEEN ASSEMBLED IN THE DEPARture Lounge, the obligatory flight delay was announced. The man with the children sank on to a couch and closed his eyes as though seeking unconsciousness. Hortense opened her hat-box, removed two comic books and a doll for comfort, closed it again and, hugging the doll, opened a comic. Marvin was immediately immersed in a magazine of his own, when he tilted it to turn a page, Stacey caught a glimpse of the title: *Scientific American*. Precocious, too, it seemed.

She barricaded herself behind her own magazines, steadfastly ignoring the hopeful signals emanating from the academic. She should be safe once they boarded the plane; she had noticed his reproachful look when she asked for a seat in the Smoking Section. Unfortunately it did not appear to have discouraged him completely; perhaps he thought he might make a convert if he had a chance to talk to her. Another good reason for escaping his attentions.

The other passengers milled about, exchanged resigned complaints, or retreated behind their own supplies of reading matter. Eventually the plane would arrive and they would be allowed to board it, there was no use wasting energy in indignation.

At last the announcement came. They went out to the waiting jumbo jet and boarded quietly, after yet another last-minute delay.

First Class was nearly empty. There were a few people who had been on board from some previous starting-point of the journey and Stacey noticed with surprise that two men she had vaguely been aware of in the airport were already aboard and seated, although she was one of the first into the section and they had not been ahead of her.

Surprisingly, the man and his two children were also travelling first, she had mentally tagged them as Economy Class. Not so surprisingly, the model sauntered down the aisle and claimed an aisle seat across from her and the well-to-do matron settled in just behind the model.

Still looked reproachful, the academic took a seat in the section labelled "Non-smoking." He had the air, however, of one who might issue an invitation to the upstairs cocktail bar at the slightest encouragement. Stacey resolved to light one of her own rare cigarettes as soon as the "No Smoking" sign was extinguished to further discourage him.

The whine of the motors changed key; the announcement lights flashed on; the jet quivered, then began moving down the runway with increasing speed. There were the heartstopping moments while the jet left the ground and soared upward, not fighting for altitude but demanding it as a right. It was the white-knuckle brigade pressed back in their seats who were variously fighting, praying or just resigning themselves to the inevitable.

Eventually the jet levelled off, the signs darkened and the pilot's voice came over the public address system to announce the altitude, tailwind and current place of interest passing by underneath and to their left.

Breaths were exhaled, seat-belts unfastened, cigarettes lighted; the atmosphere improved perceptibly. The hostess began to move among them taking orders for drinks.

Stacey was seated by herself in the double seat immediately behind the cockpit. She put the hat-box in the empty seat beside her to discourage visitors and agreed that she would like a bourbon and ginger ale.

"Gee, Hortense—" She identified the unmistakable accents from the block of three seats behind her. "You're not going to miss it, after all. Hortense, Al, look over there. Those two guys sitting all by themselves in the middle of the row. Al, I got a good look at them at Logan—that was what I wanted to show Hortense. Al— they're handcuffed together!"

Instinctively Stacey turned her head. Unreprimanded for once for his familiarity, Marvin was cautiously pointing to the pair of men seated in solitary splendor—perhaps solitary confinement, if his information was correct—in the middle of the center block of seats. Hortense gazed at them wide-eyed, even the elegant Alistair Lord was agog.

"Which one do you think is the cop?" Marvin whispered.

It was a good question. Both men looked equally distinguished. Stockbrokers, one might have said in a snap guess as to their occupation. Business tycoons, scientists, film moguls, advertising executives, international troubleshooters for some multinational—there was nothing so inherently respectable about any profession as to preclude the possibility of criminal activity. A checkbook flourished too enthusiastically, a change of law in some foreign country, and anyone could be a criminal.

But it *would* be fascinating to know the answer to Marvin's question.

No wonder the two men had been allowed to board the plane ahead of the rest of the passengers. Even now the stewardess, with a professionally blank smile, was approaching them to ask for their drinks order. It appeared that first class was first class and they were to be treated no differently from the rest of the passengers.

"It must be a Scotland Yard man extraditing a criminal," Alistair Lord said softly. "I don't recognize either of them, but then I'm not particularly knowledgeable about these matters."

"They're both the same size," Marvin said with dissatisfaction. "Usually it's the big guy who's the cop."

"Size doesn't necessarily mean a thing," Alistair Lord spoke with the quick defensiveness of a man who secretly wished he were a few inches taller. "Napoleon was below average height."

"And he was a good general," Marvin agreed. "My father said so.

"General Birnbaum ought to be the expert," Alistair admitted drily.

So he was not Marvin's father himself. Without thinking, she turned her head still farther and found herself crossing glances with Alistair Lord. It was too sudden and something in his gaze made her feel like an eavesdropper—which, or course, she was. And he knew it. Blushing, she turned away hurriedly.

"Your bourbon and ginger ale." The stewardess appeared with her order, smiling the same blank smile. "There'll be champagne with your dinner, which will be served in about half an hour." Presumably this was a warning not to go overboard and order a second drink. It was tactfully phrased so as not to imply criticism of any who were absolutely determined to gain more altitude than the plane; airlines could not run the risk of insulting anyone prepared to pay first-class fares these days.

"Thank you." Stacey produced a bland smile of her own and the stewardess wheeled her trolley to the next seat.

"Why can't I have a bullshot?" Marvin demanded behind her. "I've paid my fare—anyway, my father has."

"If you don't behave," Alistair Lord said with deadly quietness, "I'll give you a shot, all right. Why can't you behave yourself, like Hortense? She doesn't give any trouble. What would you like, Hortense?"

"Pernod," Hortense said firmly.

Stacey turned in time to see the air hostess's smile glaze over.

"They'll both have orange juice," Alistair said, with equal firmness. "And if you'd like to add a jigger of paregoric, I wouldn't blame you a bit. In fact, I'd be most obliged."

"I'm afraid, sir," the hostess began, "we don't have any—"

"All right, all right," he said. "It was just a passing thought."

"And would you like orange juice, sir?"

"God, no!" He shuddered. "I'll take gin. That's why I'm in the Smoking section—I need all the crutches I can get!"

She dispensed their drinks with unseemly haste and moved across the aisle to the model, who required diet cola.

Who was she? Casually Stacey picked up her copy of *Vogue* and, trying not to make it too obvious, turned to the page which gave that information.

Of course. Imelda Butler. This, it seemed, was her sixth *Vogue* cover (other magazines weren't counted); she travelled frequently to model the Paris, Florence and London collections; and there were plans afoot to star her in a feature film soon.

That question settled, she discarded the magazine on top of the hat-box and took up a paperback.

"May I, madame?" Two dark intense eyes peered round the seat behind, a small hand stretched forward yearningly toward the magazine. Hortense, too, had noticed their illustrious fellow passenger.

"Help yourself," Stacey smiled.

A shy, fleeting smile answered her and the magazine was whisked away.

"Marvin, look!" There was the sound of pages being turned excitedly. "You see?" Hortense's voice rose, pronouncing her verdict. "This is the most interesting plane I have ever travelled on. Usually they are all *diplomatique*—so dull!"

"MATS isn't so hot, either," Marvin admitted. "In fact, the Army's pretty dull all round."

Two world-weary sighs deplored their lot.

It seemed that the stewardesses had barely finished serving drinks when the trolleys began rolling along the aisles again accompanied by the clatter of trays. A film had been promised after dinner for those who were willing to remove to the rear compartment. Since it would look exceedingly eccentric to carry a hat-box to watch a film, Stacey had no option but to remain in her seat. In any case, the film did not sound particularly interesting and she was so tired it was possible that she might even be able to get some sleep.

The champagne was excellent and the dinner seemed no worse than usual. Headphones had also been given out for those who wished them, but Stacey found the conversation behind her more amusing than the music selection announced in the in-flight programme. She suspected others did as well. Only the two men handcuffed together had so far availed themselves of the opportunity the headphones presented of cutting off the rest of the world.

"Al, you don't want your sugar, do you?" Marvin's voice rose insistently. "Can I have it? You don't really want it, do you?"

"Oh, all right," Alistair sighed. "Anything for a quiet life. Isn't your drink sweet enough for you?"

"I don't want it for my drink." Marvin carefully stored the sachet of sugar away in one of his pockets. "I just want it. I collect sugar." He looked around for more likely victims.

"Excuse me—" He wriggled free of his seat and crossed the aisle to Imelda Butler. "You don't use sugar, do you? Girls usually don't, because of staying thin. Could I have yours, please?"

"I guess so." She handed it over to him, looking amused.

"Thank you." His eyes fell on Stacey and he started toward her purposefully.

"Help yourself," she said, as his hand twitched covetously over her tray.

"Here, sonny," the matronly woman called from farther down the aisle, holding out her unopened packet and jingling an over-loaded gold charm bracelet at him to attract his attention. "You can have mine, too, if you want."

"Gee, thanks." Once the ice had been broken, other passengers began proffering their sugar. Face alight, Marvin moved up and down the aisles with all the avidity of a born collector.

"Why don't you just ask the stewardess for some if

you wanted a souvenir?'' Alistair asked as Marvin returned to his seat, juggling so many packets of sugar that they threatened to slip from his grasp.

''I'm going to.'' Marvin sounded preoccupied as he distributed his booty in various pockets. ''But they only give you one or two and think they're doing you a great big favor.'' He spoke with the voice of long experience. ''You get more this way.''

''You do this often, do you?'' The nuances had not escaped Alistair Lord.

''I like sugar.'' Marvin still seemed abstracted.

''You must.'' He was amused. ''Tell me, did the boys call you 'Sugar' at school?''

''Not more than once,'' Marvin said grimly.

''Is that why you were expelled from the military academy?''

''Not this time.'' Marvin shrugged off the question. ''Listen, Al—'' It might have been a conscious change of subject or it might not.

''Al, Hortense, take a look at that guy in gray there at the back. *He's* handcuffed, too. He doesn't think I saw them, but he was trying to cut his meat just as I went to ask him for his sugar and I couldn't help noticing. He's handcuffed to his briefcase.''

Hortense whimpered with excitement; the passengers on Flight 1302 were continuing to live up to her expectations.

But had the boy's imagination been overstimulated by the presence of the policeman and his prisoner, so that he was seeing handcuffs where perhaps only the steel wristband of a watch existed?

"You sit here." Evidently Alistair Lord was wondering the same thing. "I'll be right back."

Stacey felt the back of her seat jump as he knocked against it in his haste.

"Sorry," he apologized perfunctorily. She nodded without turning, although it was unlikely that he noticed.

He was not gone long. "It's all right," he reported to Marvin upon returning. "The man is the Queen's Messenger, he has the silver greyhound on his lapel."

"What does that mean?" Marvin asked.

"It means he's on government business, carrying despatches or something in that briefcase. He's a courier."

Like herself. The plane was full of them, Stacey thought. She began to wonder how many others were not what they appeared.

"*Secret* papers?" Marvin asked. "Something spies would like to get hold of? They'd have to cut off his hand to get that briefcase away from him, though, wouldn't they?"

"Marvin," Alistair Lord said wearily. "The man is probably carrying nothing more exciting than a list of delegates to some Commonwealth Conference or other. It's just a custom to have the briefcase chained to his wrist."

"Yeah," Marvin said with growing enthusiasm. "But suppose it was more than that, something really Top Secret and somebody hi-jacked the plane with all of us aboard just to get at him?"

"Marvin, don't you and Hortense want to see the film? You'd better get back there. It's nearly time for it to start."

"Okay," Marvin said, having thought it over. "Probably

nothing will happen till everybody's asleep and we're past the point of no return anyway.''

"Marvin—" Alistair warned.

"Okay, okay, we're going. Aren't you coming?"

"No, Marvin," Alistair said patiently. "I thought I'd take advantage of the peace and quiet to snatch a little sleep. I'm going no farther than across the aisle to those unoccupied seats so I can stretch out and you won't disturb me when you return."

It was a good idea, Stacey decided. The dinner and drinks, plus the hypnotic whine of the engines, were making her feel sleepy herself. She had not slept much last night. She could at least rest, if not sleep, for a little while. She turned off the reading light over her seat and closed her eyes.

CHAPTER 4

OVER THE BACKGROUND DRONE OF THE JET, STACEY gradually became aware that muffled giggles and whispers had been teasing at the fringe of her consciousness for some time. Was the film over already? What time was it?

She blinked at her watch, then realized it wouldn't be very helpful. It still showed the time in Boston, but it would be five hours later in London. Meanwhile, they were at some mid-point where time was meaningless.

Most of the passengers seemed to be asleep. Even as she glanced around, a particularly explosive giggle made Alistair Lord twitch suspiciously, then brought him wide awake. He stared across the aisle, aghast.

"Hortense!" It was a muted roar. "Where did you get those? Oh my God! Hortense!" He leaped across the aisle, staring about at the other passengers in horror.

Hortense began to sniffle, then sob.

"Whose are they?" With an obvious effort, he brought a coaxing note into his voice. "Tell Alistair, Hortense. Where did you get that stuff?"

Instinctively, Stacey knew. She hardly had to confirm by a quick glance that her hat-box was missing from the seat beside her. She stood up sharply and turned to look down at the scene in the row behind.

In the semi-darkness of the cabin, it looked as though flames were leaping in a halo around Hortense's small head. More flames flickered uncertainly at her throat, on her arms, on her fingers, from her tiny shoulders. The Orpington Bequest, in all it's glory, was sliding about on a frame much too small to counterbalance it. If Hortense were startled into sudden movement, a bracelet or ring might slide off and roll into some dark corner and be lost. Or the tiara might tumble from her head and be damaged.

"Hortense—" Alistair began threateningly.

"It's all right," Stacey said quietly. "It's mine. That is," she qualified, "the museum's."

"Oh my God!" Alistair said again. "I can't tell you how sorry I am. I don't know how this could have happened. I was asleep—'' He laughed bitterly. "You'd think it would be safe to sleep for a couple of hours on a plane, wouldn't you? The kids couldn't get off and run away. There didn't *seem* to be any mischief they could get into. I do apologize. I'm frightfully sorry—''

He snatched at Hortense's arm and began stripping the jewels from her. Hortense twisted away, struggling to retain her prizes.

"*Non!*" she shrieked. "*Non!*"

"Shhh—it's all right." Stacey came around to join them, intent on soothing the child. "Don't cry, Hortense."

"And you—'' Alistair turned his embarrassed fury on Marvin. "Hortense is just a baby, you're old enough to know better. How could you stand by and let her do such a thing?"

"How was I to know?" Marvin was the picture of injured innocence. "That hat-box looked just like the one Hortense has. I couldn't tell the difference until she had it open. And—'' he clinched his defense—"she opened it with her *own* key!"

Damn Gordon and his cheese paring economies! Of course, all the hat boxes would have had the same key and lock. Why couldn't he have purchased a decent piece of luggage?

"I am *not* a baby?" Hortense tackled the deadliest insult first. "And I thought it was *my* hat-box. *Enfin*—'' Her voice rose in a wail of self-justification. "Madame *told* me I could help myself!"

"That's right," Marvin seconded quickly. "She told me I could help myself, too. She shouldn't say things if she doesn't mean them."

"This was not what she had in mind—" Alistair spoke between clenched teeth. "And you both know it! You will both apologize at once to Miss—Miss—"

"Orpington," Stacey supplied.

"How do you do?" Automatically he extended a hand which contained one of the bracelets. "I'm sorry we're not meeting in pleasanter circumstances. I'm Alistair Lord."

"I know," Stacey said, and blushed. She had not meant to betray the extent of her eavesdropping. She removed the bracelet from it and shook the outstretched hand.

"Oh?" He seemed obscurely gratified. "Did you catch the play? You must have been quick, it didn't last long."

Stacey was saved from having to reply as Hortense meekly took off the tiara and held it out to her.

"I'm sorry, madame," she sobbed. "I only wanted to try them on. They were so pretty."

"We were going to put them back," Marvin said. "And nobody would have ever known. Only—" he gave Alistair an unfriendly look—"only *you* had to wake up just then."

Alistair was not the only one who had awakened. Stacey saw with concern that curious faces were turned in their direction. She had the feeling that others had been watching, but had glanced away quickly just before she looked at them. Only the Scotland Yard man and his prisoner seemed not to have been disturbed by the commotion. But then, each of them was trained in his own way not to betray himself.

The antithesis of Alistair, in fact. Now that she had the essential clue, she could see the relaxed elegance of his bearing, the almost-too-handsome face behind which was the training which now automatically projected his emotions as surely as though he were framed by a proscenium arch.

"Where is Miss Orpington's hat-box?" Right now, Alistair was projecting anger, exasperation and apology. It was obviously not his fault that the play had closed.

"I got it." A subdued Marvin brought it out from underneath his seat. "We were going to put everything back in, honest we were, just the way it was."

"Nothing should ever have been taken out. Hurry up, Hortense. Give Miss Orpington the rest of her jewels."

"Actually," Stacey began, "they belong to the museum. I'm just acting as a courier—"

A sharp intake of breath swung her round. The stewardess was leaning over the back of the seat, eyes wide with admiration—and avarice.

"They're going on display at the Royal Arts Museum next week," Stacey finished. "As centerpiece to the exhibition of Duvanov's work."

"That's one exhibition I'm going to make a point to see," the stewardess said. "Imagine—all that being on my plane!" Her eyes did not leave the jewels as Hortense reluctantly removed them, piece by piece.

Stacey tossed an absent mechanical smile toward the stewardess, wishing she would go away. There was nothing she could do and she was only adding to the confusion of the scene.

"Is everything there?" Alistair was obviously in dread of the answer. "She hasn't lost anything, has she?"

"I don't think so," Stacey said. "I'll have to check the inventory to be sure." It was an automatically evasive answer. To admit her complete familiarity with the Orpington Bequest might be to invite more questions.

Hortense, now divested of every bit of her splendor, burst into fresh sobs.

With a ferocious glare, Alistair snatched the hat-box from Marvin and flipped open the lid. Still maintaining an air of injured dignity, Marvin handed Hortense a slightly grubby handkerchief and patted her shoulder.

"You shouldn't have shouted at Hortense," he said righteously. "It upsets her."

"Just sit down," Alistair said. "And don't either of you dare move until Miss Orpington makes sure she has everything."

"I'm sure I have." Stacey tumbled the jewels loosely into the hat-box and took it back to her own seat where she ostentatiously checked each item against the inventory and tucked it back into its proper compartment.

Alistair hovered over the back of her seat as she did so. To her annoyance, the stewardess also seemed reluctant to move away, but watched mesmerized as the folds of black velvet enveloped the gleaming gems.

"There!" Stacey finished her task and put a check mark beside the final item of the inventory. "All present and accounted for."

"No thanks to my little charges, I'm afraid," Alistair said. "I'll bet you could cheerfully kill us all, couldn't you?"

"Well," Stacey said, "the idea *was* to get the jewels from one country to another as inconspicuously as possible."

"And now—" He whistled softly. "You couldn't be more conspicuous if you'd had a spotlight on you. Thanks to Hortense."

Hearing her name, Hortense renewed her sniffling.

"It can't be helped now," Stacey said. There was no point in getting paranoiac over it. After all, she comforted herself, people travelling first class were highly unlikely to be jewel thieves, even when the temptation presented itself. (It was a theory that might hold more water if there were not a man in handcuffs just a few rows to the rear. What *was* he being extradited for?)

In any case, the risk of trying to take newly-stolen jewellery through customs would surely be too high. There could be no guarantee that the thief would not be stopped in one of the random Customs inspections and caught with the impossible-to-explain loot. She herself was weighted down by the papers in her handbag regarding the jewellery. There had been much prior correspondence and she now held a temporary import license and various forms, all connected with the jewellery. Furthermore, Customs officials knew that she was arriving on this flight and would doubtless meet her and check the contents of the hat-box against the inventory. She had been hoping that such a check might be carried out in a private room—but it was immaterial now.

With a small sigh, Stacey snapped down the lid of the hat-box and locked it—with the common key.

A louder, more heartfelt sigh echoed her own and

Stacey looked up in time to see the stewardess reluctantly wrench her gaze from the hat-box and move away.

Members of the air crew were rarely stopped by Customs. Even if an alarm were to be raised, in which case it was more than likely that someone in the crew would know of a thousand hiding places where jewellery could be hidden until the search died down.

Paranoia was definitely settling in! The feeling of disorientation, due to the unearthly hour, the constant high-pitched drone of the jet engines and what it seemed was going to be an equally constant sniffling sound from Hortense in the seat behind, was quite bad enough. She shook her head, trying to clear it.

"For God's sake, shut up, Hortense!" Alistair Lord snapped. "You're keeping everyone awake."

Hortense took a deep breath and broke into renewed wailing.

"Here, honey—" There was the sound of a charm bracelet being jingled enticingly. "Come over here and see *my* jewellery."

Hortense halted in mid-wail.

"Come on—" the woman coaxed, the bracelet jingled again. "Come and see Aunt Barbie. *I'll* let you try on *my* jewellery."

Hortense moved abruptly, pushing aside Alistair Lord who was partially blocking her way by standing in the aisle. He sighed heavily.

"Just a few more hours, I keep telling myself. Just a few more hours and it will all be over. I deliver them to their respective families and then I'll be free of them both."

"What's the matter, Al? Don't you like us?" Marvin was aggrieved. "You want to get rid of us?"

"At least—" Alistair ignored Marvin, continuing to address himself to Stacey. "You're courier to inanimate objects. You don't know your luck."

"They're not your own?" Stacey blushed at his incredulous look. "I mean," she amended hastily, "I realized Marvin wasn't, but I thought possibly Hortense—"

"Never!" he said. "After this last week, I may take a solemn vow never to have any offspring. I don't think my nerves could stand it."

"Then why—? I'm sorry. It's none of my business."

"We brought a show to Broadway from the West End," he explained patiently. She had the feeling that it was not for the first time. "It had run for a year in London—it's still running now—so naturally we expected it to be a hit on Broadway, too."

"It doesn't always work out that way," Stacey said.

"So we discovered. The show closed in a fortnight. Since the English and American sides of Equity were locked in their usual mortal combat, that meant none of us could take other jobs—in the theater. A couple of the members of the cast went straight back to England, the leading lady went to Canada and got a film job there. I stayed on for a while and got some slightly illegal work doing voice-overs for television commercials. They needed an English accent and I came cheaper than an American who could do it because they knew my circumstances and worked it so that they wouldn't have to pay me residuals. Otherwise, I'd have been doing quite well by now—"

"You broke the law, Al?" Marvin had been listening with fascination and now he joined the conversation in too loud a tone. They were aware of a stir of interest in the rows behind them.

"Not really," Alistair said loudly and quickly. The interest died away. "Well, not very much," he added in a lower voice. "Only bent it enough to keep eating."

"Yeah, that's the best reason," Marvin approved. He stared at Alistair, obviously seeing him in a new light.

"Anyway," Alistair went on, "one of my friends took a job as a camp counsellor at a boys' summer camp up in the Adirondacks for the summer. One of those very expensive places where the rich send their children to get them out of their hair while schools are closed for the summer holidays—"

"It was a real dump," Marvin volunteered. "We all hated it."

"From what I've heard, Marvin, it was mutual."

"Listen, I've been thrown out of lots better places than *that*."

"And will be again, no doubt."

"Was it a military-style camp?" Stacey asked curiously.

"Naw—" Marvin picked absently at a dangling shoulder thread. "That was the place before. Most of the places before. My Dad wants me to make a career of the Army, like him, but I don't want to. I'd rather be a research scientist. I've got an enquiring mind. That's the problem. Military academies can't cope with enquiring minds. Most people can't."

"Precisely," Alistair said. "So there was my friend, trapped in this summer camp as counsellor and drama teacher to forty-three enquiring little minds. I had several letters from him threatening suicide and murder—not necessarily in that order. Then came the letter to say that they were washing their hands of Marvin—'' He broke off guiltily.

"That's all right," Marvin said generously. "You should have heard what Colonel Ratface said. That was what we called him—" Marvin answered Stacey's raised eyebrow. "It wasn't his real name."

"And what did he call you? No, never mind." Alistair passed a weary hand across his forehead. "I think I'd rather not know. Anyway—" he turned back to Stacey—"I had already been engaged to escort Hortense back to her grandmother in Paris since her school was over for the summer. So it seemed as though it would be no trouble at all to escort Marvin, too, and I could use the extra money while I looked around for a new job. It all seemed so simple. Little did I know!"

In the thoughtful silence, they could hear "Aunt Barbie" continuing to soothe Hortense with stories of the charms on her bracelet as Hortense fingered each one moodily. "Now, that one doesn't look like much, but it's interesting. They call it the Whistling Pig. Can you guess why?"

Hortense shook her head.

"Because when they've got the pipeline built, before they send oil through it, they pump this through so that they can tell if there are any leaks or breaks. And, if you're standing on the ground above, you can hear a whistling noise as it goes by underneath. The Whistling Pig, see?"

Hortense looked puzzled, but evidently decided that

her English might be somewhat at fault and did not pursue the question. The bracelet jingled as she turned to the next charm. "This one moves," she said.

"That's right. That's the Nodding Donkey. See, it goes up and down. That's what they put over a working well, once they've capped it, to do the pumping. Up and down, up and down..."

"Pig? Donkey?" Hortense gave up. "Why do you keep giving things the names of animals when you are talking about oil?"

"That's an awfully good question, honey," the woman sighed. "I'm not sure I know the answer. I suppose it's because most of the oil they found in the States in the early days was on farmland. That's when all of these things got their names. I suppose the oil men looked around for things that reminded them of something familiar—"

"And they saw the animals on the farmland." Hortense nodded gravely. "And so, the pig, the donkey..."

"And look at this one—" The woman turned to another charm. "Dan bought me that when he brought in his first big gusher. See, it's a little gusher, with diamond chips on the spray coming out of the top. Isn't it cute? He had it made specially—"

Hortense began sniffling again. It had obviously been a mistake to remind her of diamonds and the treasures she had had snatched away from her. Mere gold was not an acceptable substitute. And as for chips compared to large beautifully faceted stones... The sniffles threatened to break into full-throated sobs.

"Oh, but look at my glacier!" The command was so

sharp that both Stacey and Alistair whirled around in time to see the woman thrust an enormous diamond solitaire ring under Hortense's bemused eyes. "That was too big to fit on to a charm bracelet, so it took the place of the engagement ring Dan couldn't afford when we got married. He gave me this to commemorate his work on the Alaska Pipeline. "A big hunk of ice," he said, for all the ice I had to put up with while he was on that job." She sighed.

"The trouble with oil," her voice was reflective and resigned, "is that it seems to show up in the most Godforsaken places the world possesses." She sighed again and there was a lost world in her sigh; a world of comfortable homes, continuing friendships, permanent neighbors, roots—all the things a woman had to forfeit if she devoted her life to trying to make a home for a man who was always on the move.

"Here—" the woman said impulsively. "It's too big for you, but you can wear it for just a minute. The charm bracelet, too."

Hortense thrust out an eager hand, all grievances momentarily forgotten.

"There! Don't you look pretty now? I'll bet there isn't another little girl in town—in any airplane anywhere in the sky—who looks as pretty as you do right now."

Hortense preened, holding the glacier out in front of her, turning her hand so that the diamond caught and reflected the light.

"That's torn it!" Alistair groaned. "I shouldn't like to be the future gentleman who's going to try to keep that child in the manner to which she's becoming accustomed."

"*Good* morning!" the stewardess trilled brightly, appearing behind them. Her gaze fell on the glittering jewel Hortense held aloft and her voice faltered momentarily, but she recovered quickly.

"I'll start serving breakfast now to those of you who are awake, shall I? We'll be landing soon."

CHAPTER 5

AFTER ALL, IT WAS NEARLY AS EASY CLEARING CUStoms as Gordon had promised. At times, the Customs men explained, they asked for a substantial deposit from people temporarily importing such valuable items, to ensure that they would be re-exported again and not sold. However, in view of the nature of the exhibition and the previous correspondence, there was not much doubt about that. They would simply check the jewels against the inventory again as she left the country and that would be that. It had all been simple and friendly, with the Customs Officers obviously pleased at having a simple matter and a pretty girl to deal with, rather than some of the smuggling unpleasantness that more often fell to their lot.

She found a trolley for her luggage and pushed it toward the exit, mentally debating the choice of the airport bus to an intown terminal or a taxi direct to the hotel where she had a reservation.

Before she had decided, she saw another trolley bearing down on her, guided by Alistair Lord, with Hortense and Marvin on either side of it. Hortense's hat-box, like her own, perched atop the pile of luggage, far more mountainous than her own. Marvin must have been thrown out lock, stock and barrel.

"We just wanted to say goodbye," Alistair gasped, pulling his trolley even with hers. "And perhaps we'll meet again, if you're going to be in town a few weeks. You and I, I mean—" He forestalled a comment Marvin seemed about to make. "Where are you staying?"

She told him, since it might be rather pleasant to have a friend in the city.

"I'm delivering Marvin to General Birnbaum now," he said. "Then I come back here with Hortense and catch an afternoon plane to Paris and deliver her to her grandmother."

"Sounds like a busy day," Stacey said.

"Hey, look!"

"Don't point, Marvin," Alistair said automatically.

"But look!" In his excitement, Marvin jigged back and forth between the two trolleys, setting them rocking precariously. "Look—there are the two guys handcuffed together. I thought we'd lost them because the crew let them get off first. But there they are over there."

"For heaven's sake, don't wave to them! We're not on those terms—and don't want to be."

"I wasn't waving," Marvin said. "I just—" He whirled to defend himself against the charge, but there was not enough room between the two trolleys for such an action. He knocked against both of them and they tilted sharply.

Inevitably, the hat-boxes on top began to slide. Stacey grabbed for hers just as Hortense realized what was happening and dived with equal anxiety to reclaim her own. They collided and the hat-boxes hit the floor and began rolling.

"There we are—" Suddenly, the stewardess was in their midst, carrying her own hat-box over her arm. She swooped quickly to pick up Stacey's hat-box and restore it to her.

"Oh dear! I hope nothing got damaged—" Aunt Barbie" was also there, veering her trolley with its luggage and hat-box alongside the other trolleys. "It's such a responsibility! You're sure you've got the right one now?"

"I can assure you," the stewardess said frostily, "I gave her the right one."

"It's mine," Stacey assured them. "I've been keeping a close watch on it." The weight of the hat box reassured her.

"Don't you want to open it and make sure?"

"No—" Not here. Not in the middle of Heathrow Airport. It was bad enough to have been marked out among all the first-class passengers in the jumbo jet—it could be fatal to allow hundreds of perfect strangers a glimpse of what she was carrying. She felt her lips quirk in a smile; nobody's perfect.

"There they go!" Marvin shouted. He was still monitoring the progress of the handcuffed men as they went out of the door. "They're getting into a plain black car," he reported with disappointment. "I thought there'd be a police car waiting to pick them up."

"Not all police cars have markings here," the stewardess told him. "There are times when the police don't want to attract attention."

"That's funny," Marvin said thoughtfully. "They didn't seem to be walking so close together as they were before. You could notice it when they got in the car."

"Perhaps they've had a fight," Alistair said caustically. "Let's get a move on. I want to deliver you to Sloane Square in good time to—" He broke off as a stranger expression crossed Marvin's face. "What's the matter?"

"Nothing, Al. Nothing's the matter." A look of improbable innocence hastily replaced the expression. "Why should anything be the matter?"

"That's what I'd like to know," Alistair said suspiciously.

"Well," the stewardess said, "it's been nice meeting all of you. I hope you'll fly with us again. Have a good day." With a slight wave, she dashed through the doors and into a car which had just drawn up outside.

"Are you people taking the airport bus?" Barbara Donaldson seemed anxious to prolong their encounter, perhaps feeling daunted at the prospect of a lonely day ahead. "I thought I would."

"It's the best way," Alistair spoke directly to Stacey. "We can pick up taxis in town—it's far cheaper."

"Well . . ." Stacey allowed herself to waver, pushing her trolley into the loading bay along with theirs. "I'm *not* sure I have enough English pounds for a taxi. Not until I get to a bank this afternoon. So, perhaps—*Oh!*"

The loader caught her by surprise, whipping the luggage off the trolleys and into the dark recesses beneath the bus so quickly that she could not have anticipated it, even if her attention had not been momentarily distracted by her calculations.

"Not that one, please!" She lunged forward and retrieved her hat-box. "That's my hand baggage. I'll take it inside with me."

"I want mine, too," Hortense declared. "*That* one, there! I'll take it inside with me." Her unconscious imitation was perfect.

"You can keep mine," Barbara Donaldson said. "There's nothing in it worth bothering about. Just the layette I'm knitting for my daughter's baby—I'm going to be a grandmother, imagine!—and enough wool to finish it. Nothing of any value." She sighed. "Not even any sentimental value . . . yet."

More people came up behind them, jostling them. They turned to see Imelda Butler, who had somehow acquired a porter, direct the placement of her cases in luggage hold with an imperious sweep of her hand. She was not concerned about holding on to her hat-box, either, Stacey noted.

"I've been let down," Imelda complained. "Someone was supposed to meet me—with a car."

"The car broke down—" Someone said bitterly. "It wasn't *my* fault. I offered to get a taxi—"

"And I ought to let you! But I hate to see anybody get ripped off—even you. The bus will do." With an unseeing nod to her rapt audience, she turned and mounted the steps into the bus. Someone following in her wake.

The loader distributed their baggage checks and they all entered the bus and took their seats.

Stacey was amused that Hortense chose to sit next to her, despite Barbara Donaldson's blandishments. Evidently she had been forgiven for reclaiming her own— well, the museum's—jewellery and Hortense was going to bear no grudge. Fleetingly, she even regretted that she wouldn't see the children again. They were rather pleasant and amusing—although Alistair Lord's haggard visage bore witness that they could be extremely tiresome on a long-term basis.

Or perhaps he was looking so disgruntled because he had hoped to sit next to Stacey himself.

She would not, she thought, mind getting to know him better, either. Fortunately, it appeared that there was a good prospect of that. She pushed the thought of Gordon firmly to the back of her mind. She was on holiday— once her duty to the museum was discharged—and she was just beginning to realize how long it had been since she had had a real holiday.

She listened amiably to Hortense's chatter as the bus rolled past the factories and little houses lining the route to Central London.

They parted, each to their own taxi, with a lingering friendliness and regret. Air travel, quick and convenient though it might be, gave no one the chance to do more than establish brief contact; hardly enough to suggest a future meeting on the strength of such acquaintance, let alone establish a lasting friendship. Great-Grand-Aunt Eustacia's tales of long leisurely voyages with like-minded people who ripened into close friends were now as much legends of a golden age as family chronicles.

"I'll ring you later," Alistair said, herding his charges into their taxi.

She nodded, waved to the children and they were gone.

It was not until she got to her hotel room that she discovered she had the wrong hat-box.

She stared down at the open case with blank incredulous horror. The pert painted face of Suzette pouted up at her.

It couldn't be! Stacey reached down and picked up the doll, as though the Orpington tiara might be hidden beneath the wide satin crinoline skirt.

The painted Pierrot grinned up at her, cushioned on the soft Snoopy doll.

She picked up the acrobat doll and set him on the floor where he rocked gently in his wooden frame from the violence of the movement with which she had disturbed him. Then, the delicate balance set in motion, the Pierrot made a long lazy somersault over the balance bar of his frame and began a slow progress across the carpet.

Resisting a strong impulse to kick the Pierrot so that he bounced off the opposite wall and then to hurl Suzette and Snoopy after him, Stacey burrowed frantically down to the bottom of the hat-box. She found nothing but a jumble of comic books, coloring books, crayons, paints, airline souvenirs . . .

Damn Hortense, anyhow!

And damn Stacey, for being stupid and off-guard when

the child had sat beside her and prattled innocently on the airport bus. So sweet, so innocent—*so scheming*!

The child couldn't seriously imagine, even at her age, that she could get away with it!

Stacey chased after the Pierrot, caught it up and tossed it back into the hat-box, not caring whether she disturbed the delicate mechanism or even broke the toy completely. It would serve Hortense right! She threw Suzette and Snoopy in on top of Pierrot with unnecessary force and snapped the lid shut. There was no point in locking it.

Had Hortense done this alone or had Marvin helped her?

For a wild moment, Stacey wondered whether she could absolve Alistair Lord of any collusion. Surely he would know that they couldn't get away with stealing the Orpington Collection.

But this was his own home territory. He might also know where one could sell stolen jewellery quickly and safely, to be broken up and resold for its intrinsic value— which was not inconsiderable.

The telephone rang.

She started for it automatically, jolted out of her uneasy thoughts. Alistair had said that he would call.

Just as she put her hand on the receiver, she was struck motionless by another thought: Suppose it wasn't Alistair Lord? Suppose it was the Exhibition Organizer from the Royal Arts Museum?

How could she talk to him? How could she answer questions as to when she would deliver the Orpington Collection? How could she admit that she had lost it? How could she explain?

She pulled her hand away and moved back from the phone. It continued to ring, but she dared not answer it now.

She had to get the jewellery back before she even admitted she was in London. As for the cablegram she was supposed to send to Gordon announcing her safe arrival . . . she shuddered.

The telephone would not stop ringing. Whoever it was, was not going to give up easily.

Stacey caught up her handbag and hat-box and ran from the room.

CHAPTER 6

ONCE CLEAR OF THE HOTEL, SHE STOPPED AT A BANK to cash some travellers checks lest she run short of money before locating Alistair Lord and his charges.

Sloane Square, she had heard him say. He had to deliver Marvin to Sloane Square. It was a starting-point.

It was nearly a finishing-point. She had envisaged a small tidy garden square, perhaps surrounded by iron railings and with a gate to which residents had their own keys. The sort of place she had seen in English films, surrounded by houses, a neighborhood in itself.

The reality was an open space in the center of a

commercial area, boundaried by a department store, a hotel, a theater, an underground station and shops, shops, shops. She stood on the corner by the underground station and stared about with dismay. How could she find anyone here?

The magnitude of the task swept over her and she felt a weakness at her knees. But fainting was a luxury she could not afford. Time was too short.

There were streets leading off from the Square in all directions. Long, tree-shaded avenues with old red blocks of Victorian vintage. Another long—well, she'd call it an avenue, but the street sign said "King's Road"—led off from the shops beyond the theater with more modern houses lining it. Straight ahead of her, the avenue, road, whatever, continued into the distance with stores lining both sides and probably could be safely ruled out.

She took a deep breath, concentrated, then turned back into the Tube station. When in doubt, begin with the obvious and work your way outward from there.

There was a Birnbaum in the telephone directory with an address in Lower Sloane Street, but no military rank given. She tried several other spellings, but that remained the only one in the Sloane Square area.

She noted down the address and, once outside, found it without undue difficulty. A smiling couple, leaving the building as she mounted the steps, obligingly held the door open for her so that she had no need to ring the bell and warn them of her arrival. She smiled in return and swept past the couple as though sure of her ground. A quick scan of the Entryphone information had told her that her prey was located in Flat 22.

As she approached the flat, it sounded as though World War III had broken out behind its closed door. She had to ring the bell several times before a lull in hostilities allowed it to be heard. The door was then thrown open and a barely-recognizable face appeared in the opening to demand:

"Yes? What do *you* want?"

"My hat-box," Stacey said crisply. "Immediately. Before I call the police."

"Oh my God! It's you!" Alistair Lord fell back, allowing her to enter. "*What* did you say?"

"My hat-box," Stacey repeated, stepping into the hallway. "Immediately!" She thought of adding *please*, but decided that it would be excessive.

"HORTENSE!" A trained voice at full power is an awesome thing. Alistair Lord would obviously never have any trouble in making himself heard in the farthest reaches of the largest theater without a microphone. "HORTENSE!"

Stacey winced and moved back. He sounded genuinely horrified and concerned. But then he was a professional actor.

Hortense's face peered apprehensively around the corner at the end of the hallway. It disappeared almost immediately and was replaced by Marvin's.

"You don't have to yell at Hortense," he said, "just because you're mad at me."

"This has nothing to do with you, Marvin." Alistair paused and appeared to be listening to what he had just said. "At least, I don't think it has," he amended. "Miss Orpington wants her hat-box back."

Marvin disappeared too, and there was silence in the flat.

"You'd better come down here." Alistair led the way to the large reception room where the children lurked. "We'll have to straighten this out."

"We certainly will," Stacey said grimly.

The large room was shadowed and somehow ghostly. In the gloom produced by partly-drawn curtains and darkening clouds outside, it took Stacey a moment to find Hortense. She spotted Marvin first. He was standing defensively in front of a large armchair. Half-hidden in the chair behind him was Hortense.

"All right, Hortense," Alistair Lord said, dangerously quiet. "Go and bring Miss Orpington her hat-box."

"*Non*!" Hortense peeked briefly around Marvin. "I do not have it!"

"Yes, you have." Stacey intervened, realizing that Hortense might possibly be innocent. "And I have yours. I don't know how they got mixed up, but they did."

"*Non*!" Hortense drew her knees up under her chin, curled her arms around them and hunched there, mute and glowering.

"I suppose," Alistair said, obviously slightly shaken by Hortense's obduracy, "there couldn't be some mistake?"

Silently Stacey set the hat box on the coffee table and flipped back the lid. Suzette smirked insanely out at the audience gathered round.

"*Non*!" Hortense protested again, not moving.

"Marvin," Alistair Lord spoke with deceptive patience. "Perhaps *you'd* be kind enough to bring Miss Orpington's case in here for her."

"Sure, Al." Subdued for once, Marvin moved off into the farther recesses of the flat.

"Thank you," Stacey said, then added thoughtfully. "Alistair, was it you who telephoned me about an hour ago at the hotel?"

"Actually, no—" He sketched a gesture of distracted apology. "Does it look as though it might have been? I'm sorry, but I'm afraid I've had other things to worry about."

More relaxed now that she was about to regain possession of the Orpington Bequest, Stacey looked around the room and discovered the reason for its ghostly appearance.

Except for the small island they inhabited in the center, the furniture was shrouded in dust sheets.

"But—?" She looked at him in sympathetic dismay. The place was clearly uninhabited and had been for some time.

"Exactly," he said. "Now what am I to do?" He took a despairing turn around the coffee table. "I'm responsible for these children, for Marvin. *In loco parentis*, as it were. Oh, it was all good clean fun, at first. I thought of it as a week of Repertory in *Goodbye, Mr. Chips*. I could deal with the situation on that basis. But now—" he swept out an arm to encompass the room.

Hortense watched him solemnly.

"What am I to do?" he asked wildly. "What?"

"*I'm* all right." Marvin came back into the room carrying the hat-box. "I keep telling you, Al. The deep-freeze is full of food, there are plenty of restaurants around here and I've got my travellers checks. You don't hafta bother about me any more. I keep telling you."

"That's right, Marvin," Alistair said. "But you didn't tell me until we'd arrived here, did you?" His voice began to rise. "You didn't tell me before we left the States that there'd be no one here to care for you. That they weren't expecting you. That General Birnbaum was away on NATO exercises at an unspecified place for an unspecified length of time."

"Why should I tell you?" Marvin registered injured innocence. "For all I knew, you mighta been a spy!"

Alistair's hand twitched dangerously before he managed to control himself. It appeared that Mr. Chips was going to be one of his shorter roles—and one in which he wished no return engagement.

"Give me that!" He contented himself with snatching the hat-box from Marvin and handed it over to Stacey. "There you are," he said. "I can't tell you how sorry I am about this whole terrible shambles."

"Thank you," Stacey said coldly. Just to impress the seriousness of it, she took the inventory from her handbag, set the hat-box ostentatiously on the coffee table beside the other one, unlocked it and raised the lid slowly and carefully, hoping that Hortense had not disturbed the contents in any way that might damage them.

She looked down on a froth of white and pale yellow wool.

Incredulously, she plunged both hands into the hatbox, burrowing through the unresisting soft wool to the hard bottom of the case.

When she withdrew her hands a tiny white baby

bootee, threaded with pale lemon ribbon, feel to the floor at her feet.

"You see?" Hortense spoke triumphantly. "I *told* you I did not have Madame's case!"

"Oh my God!" Alistair Lord slumped to the floor beside the coffee table as though his legs would no longer hold him up. He stared down at the baby bootee as though he were seeing beyond it into a future of criminal proceedings, jail, and the loss of reputation and career.

Stacey sank down on to the coffee table, her own knees refusing to support her any longer. She, too, could not look away from that tiny white bootee, although it had begun to blur as her gaze lost focus and she began to consider her own position.

She could never show her face in Thringsby again! How could she go back and admit that she had lost the Orpington Bequest?

Worse—The realization swept over her. Would she be believed?

The full import of Gordon's peculiar behavior struck her with an impact it had not had at the time.

Those questions! Those odd insinuating questions: *Stacey, are you sure you don't mind? . . . Doesn't it ever bother you? . . . The thought that they ought to be yours? . . . Would have been yours . . . if only . . .*

Gordon himself had not fully trusted her, had been half-afraid that he had been putting too much temptation into her path.

How, then, could she expect the citizens of Thringsby to give her the benefit of the doubt?

Oh, they would never openly accuse her to her face. They would pay lip service to whatever story she chose to put about. But there would always be a sardonic quirk to certain lips and a glint—sometimes censorious, sometimes approving—lurking behind the half-lowered lids of the eyes that would be constantly appraising her...

No, she could never show her face in Thringsby again. And that, of itself, would damn her.

More immediate than that—She remembered the pleasant interview with the Customs officials (would they be so pleasant at the next interview?) She could not even leave England unless she took the Orpington Bequest out with her. Otherwise, she would be liable for untold thousands in import duty for the gems she would presumably have sold while here.

Whatever way she looked at it, she was in the most appalling trouble she had ever known in her life.

"Oh my God!" Unconsciously, she echoed Alistair.

"You mean all that millions of dollars' worth of stuff has been stolen?" Marvin spoke with the zest which could lead him to an early grave. "Hadn't we better call the cops?"

"NO!" Alistair and Stacey spoke as one.

"There's just been some terrible mix-up," Stacey pleaded. "I'll have to get hold of Mrs. Donaldson now. She must have the other hat-box. And," she added desperately, "she must want her own hat-box back."

"*I* wouldn't if I was her," Marvin said emphatically. "I'd swap a lot of old knitting for an armload of jewellery any day!"

Hortense's head bobbed up and down in endorsement of Marvin's pragmatic view.

"When we feel the need of your opinion, Marvin," Alistair said, "we'll ask for it."

"Okay for you." Marvin shrugged elaborately and turned his back on them. "Maybe when you're interested," he threw back over his shoulder, "you might ask me what hotel Mrs. Donaldson is staying at."

Alistair's hand descended to grasp his collar just before he cleared the doorway.

CHAPTER 7

THE TAXI TURNED DOWN A SIDE STREET AND DREW UP in front of a hotel whose very unobtrusiveness suggested a tariff beyond the ordinary mortal's pocketbook.

"No—" Alistair paid the fare, waving away Stacey's offer—"I'm afraid this is our fault—and our responsibility. I'll take care of it."

Hortense gave a token repentant sniffle, but her eyes were bright with excitement and interest. She was not at all displeased with the adventure unfolding.

"That's right, Al." Marvin was frankly enthusiastic. "Put it all on the bill. My Dad will pay."

Tight-lipped, Alistair accepted the minimum of change

from the cab-driver and waved them towards the hotel. The children closed around Stacey, Alistair brought up the rear, and they entered the quiet luxurious family hotel looking,' she suddenly realized, very much like a family.

"Yes, sir?" The reception clerk beamed upon them. "Two rooms or a suite?"

"Mrs. Donaldson," Alistair said, ignoring the implications. "Mrs. Barbara Donaldson, please."

"I'm not sure she's in." The clerk reached for the telephone. "Was she expecting you?"

"Tante Barbie will be pleased to see me," Hortense said spontaneously, before anyone else could speak.

"Ah, of course." The clerk's face softened into a smile. This was a family hotel and it was good to see families appearing again. It was not alwasy the case in these days of transients and tourists.

"She's in Room 414. Shall I ring and let her know you're here?"

"Don't bother," Alistair said. "We'll go straight up." He led them across the lobby to the lifts before the clerk could protest.

Given different circumstances, Stacey could have spent an afternoon just roaming those hotel corridors, which were lined with early Victorian and Georgian paintings and items of antique furniture good enough to be museum pieces. Hortense, too, seemed disposed to linger, but Alistair swept them along and rapped sharply on the door of 414.

"Yes?" Barbara Donaldson opened her door, the expression of mild expectancy on her face giving way to one of blank amazement as she saw them all standing there.

"There's been some awful mix-up." Alistair said abruptly. "May we come in and try to straighten it out? I'm terribly afraid Hortense has made off with your case."

Hortense, seeing that the blame was about to be placed on her shoulders again, gave a preliminary sniffle.

"Come in." Barbara Donaldson stepped back and they crowded into the room. She glanced dubiously at the hat-box Stacey was carrying.

"I don't really see how they could have got mixed up," she said. "Butt I suppose it's possible. Things were pretty confused for a while there at the airport."

"They certainly were," Stacey said grimly. "And when I got to my hotel, I found I had Hortense's hat-box instead of my own."

Hortense whimpered. "I did not do it. I thought it was mine. I would not part with Suzette and Pierrot and Snoopy."

"You have them back now," Alistair said impatiently. "But Miss Orpington still doesn't have her own hat-box."

"Oh, heavens!" Barbara Donaldson was aghast as she realized the problem. "You mean—all that jewellery is missing?" She began to look uncomfortable. "But why have you come here? I can assure you I'd never—"

"Hortense had *your* hat-box." Stacey cut off a protest of innocence that wouldn't take long to turn into indignation at being suspected at all. She snapped open the hat-box and lifted the lid to prove it.

"Why, I can't believe it." Barbara Donaldson fell back from the froth of lacy knitting as though reluctant to touch it. "I'd have sworn that was over in the corner. And you mean *I've* got your—? Oh heavens!" She turned and dashed to the far corner of the room where she pulled the hat-box from the pile of luggage.

"Here!" She thrust it at Stacey. "I don't want it! I mean, I'd love to have those lovely things, of course. But I certainly had no idea—"

"It's all right." Stacey's hands closed thankfully around the hat-box but, as Barbara Donaldson relinquished her own hold, Stacey's heart dipped abruptly. Surely this hat-box was just a fraction too light . . . ?

Heedless now of the other woman's sensitivity, Stacey snapped open the lid. While they were all staring incredulously, Hortense began wailing afresh.

"Shut up, Hortense," Alistair said absently.

"I didn't *do* it," Hortense howled.

"No one said you did." But the response was automatic and lacking in conviction. "So here we are, but where are we?" he asked Stacey softly.

"I don't know." Stacey sank down on the edge of the bed, the hat-box in her lap. She stared down at four cartons of duty-free cigarettes, four cartons of brandy miniatures and an assorted jumble of airline supplies, including a box of individual sugar packets.

"That's certainly an odd boxful to be carrying around," Barbara said. "But whose could it be?" She bent over Stacey and began rummaging about in the hat-box. There were several sheets of scribbled notes at the bottom and a small diary.

"The stewardess," Stacey said. "*She* had a hat-box, too. And," she added bitterly, "she was so *helpful* at the airport when the trolleys tilted and the luggage spilled off.''

"That was my fault," Marvin said ruefully. "You didn't have anything to do with that, Hortense."

But it was because of Hortense that everyone knew what was in Stacey's hat-box.

"Lola Smith," Barbara Donaldson read out. She had opened the diary and found the relevant page. "82 Walburga Mansions, Chis-wick." She flipped through the other pages with growing disappointment.

"There's nothing else personal in this at all," she complained. "It's just notes of what flights she's been assigned to and things like that."

"It's an appointments diary," Alistair explained. "Presumably, if she kept a personal diary, it would be bigger and she might also be reluctant to carry it around with her." He looked at the spoils in the hat-box. "Very reluctant."

"Well, at least we have her address," Stacey said. With a weary sigh, she struggled to her feet again.

"You're not going to chase over to Chis-wick, wherever that is?" Barbara was scandalized. "Why don't you just call the police and report it to them?"

"NO!" From Hortense to Stacey, they spoke with one voice.

"Oh, but it would be so much easier," Barbara protested.

"Would it?" Alistair shook his head. "There's every good chance that we can still sort this out quietly. There *was* a terrible shambles at the airport. This could all be an innocent blunder. If it is, Miss Smith—" he glanced at the hat-box—"won't thank us for bringing her fairly innocent pilfering to the attention of the authorities. If it isn't—'' he shrugged—''we can consider calling the police when we're sure of that.''

''Well . . .'' She was almost convinced.

Seeing that they were winning, Hortense gave a forlorn sniff. ''They will think it is all my fault,'' she whimpered. ''They will put me in a cell and try to make me confess. They will question me and question me—and I will never see *Maman* again.'' Carried away by her own pathetic picture, she burst into tears.

''Now, now, honey, they'd never do that.'' Barbara threw her arms around Hortense and rocked her comfortingly. ''Don't let all this upset you so much.''

''They might not imprison Hortense,'' Alistair said cleverly. ''But they'd certainly put the rest of us through a fairly rigorous questioning. We'd be delayed and out of action for as long as it took them to get to what they thought the bottom of it might be.''

''Delayed?'' Barbara raised her head, no longer solely concerned with Hortense. ''But I only have two days in London. I have to join Dan . . . In Abu Dhabi. I haven't any time to spare.''

''I doubt if they'll consult you about your wishes. Remember, there's a considerable fortune gone missing. They'll have a lot of questions—and a lot of checking to do on the answers. It could take a considerable length of time.''

''You're right,'' Barbara said. ''We mustn't bring the police into this. Dan will kill me if I do anything to mess up his arrangements.''

While they argued, Stacey glanced over the scrawled

notes on the loose sheets of paper. They appeared to be an impromptu list of the first-class passengers with home addresses. Presumably such information would be duplicated in the airline files but, for some reason of her own, Lola Smith had found it helpful to have it at her fingertips during the flight.

With a shrug, Stacey dropped the sheets back into the hat-box and fastened the lid. All eyes were immediately upon her.

"Where are you going?" Marvin asked.

Hortense sidled up beside her.

"Look," Stacey said. "It's been terribly kind of you to help me out like this, but I must go on and find the stewardess and get my belongings back. Thank you so much for all you've—"

"Don't be an idiot," Alistair said. "I'm coming with you."

"That's right," Marvin endorsed. "We're coming with you."

"I really can't take up any more of your time—" Stacey began firmly.

"Actually—" Alistair regarded Marvin without favor. "I wasn't thinking of all of us going."

"Why not?" Marvin protested. "We're all in this together, aren't we? I can help her too."

"*Oui*," Hortense said. "I help too."

"Besides—" Marvin was struck by a new suspicion. "What were you going to do with us while you went off with her? Were you going to abandon us all alone in a strange city?"

"Actually, I rather thought that possibly Mrs. Donaldson wouldn't mind—?"

"Think again," Barbara Donaldson said crisply. "I'm coming with you. After all, I was the one who got landed with that young lady's hat-box. I ought to be the one to give it back to her and explain. And maybe," she added thoughtfully, "assure her that I didn't examine it too closely."

"See here," Alistair said. "We can't all go."

"Why not?" Marvin asked. "We can all fit into a taxi and it won't take any time at all. Besides," he added darkly, "if you try to leave us, I'll call the cops and tell them you kidnapped me and then abandoned me."

"*Oui*," Hortense corroborated happily. "He kidnapped me too."

"My God, that brat would *do* it," Alistair groaned.

"Well, I agree with him," Barbara said. "You can't leave kids that age to their own devices. We might as well bring them along. It can't do any harm."

"Now, wait a minute," Stacey said. "Don't I have anything to say about this?"

"Not really," Alistair said. "We're all involved, you see. Suspects, if you like. Oh, don't deny it—I saw that look in your eye as you charged through the door. The only way we can really prove our innocence and be sure that you've got the right hat-box is to go with you and *make* sure."

"In fact," Barbara Donaldson said thoughtfully, "it might be a good idea for you to keep out of it this time round. She might not have looked in the hat-box. She thinks she knows what's in it, so she wouldn't bother to open it until she wanted to use the stuff inside—or sell it. If I've got her hat-box, she'll assume she's got mine, and it would probably be safer to let her think so. If she realized she had all that jewellery, she might not be so willing to part with it—given her taking little ways."

"All right." Stacey surrendered. It was not so much the strength of their arguments—although Barbara Donaldson certainly had an excellent point—it was a sudden feeling of urgency, bordering on panic, sweeping over her that decided her. What if it wasn't an innocent mistake? What if Miss Smith had deliberately switched hat-boxes? "But, please, let's hurry!"

CHAPTER 8

WALBURGA MANSIONS WAS A LARGE VICTORIAN RED-brick block of flats occupying one entire side of a genuine garden square. Narrow arched mock-Gothic windows gave a secretive look to the upper and lower floors; in the middle, the architects' enthusiasm or the builders' money had diminished and ordinary french windows opened out on to small iron-railed balconies. Some of these boasted tubs of flowering plants and hanging baskets. It seemed a curiously old-fashioned place to live for someone who had seemed as modern and stylish as Lola Smith.

There appeared to be no doorman available, although a hooded porter's chair in the spacious entry hall suggested that there had been such a functionary back in the days of the building's original grandeur. A notice board supplied the information which flats were on which floor. This information was further supplemented by a painted "In/Out" beside each flat number with a wooden slide which moved to obliterate either the In or Out and let the prospective caller know whether it was likely to be worth the effort to go up to the flat. From the look of the board, however, everyone in the block was Out—unlikely in the case of a stewardess who had just come off duty after an all-night flight. Either the board had not been utilized in years, or the inhabitants chose not to advertise there whereabouts in case of unwelcome callers.

A faded lift with flaking red leather panels alternating with narrow clouded mirrors carried them to the fifth floor. The corridor was long and narrow, closing in on itself in sharp sudden bends. The lighting was dim. Again, there was a strange secretive feeling about it. This was a place where people "kept themselves to themselves" and considered the attitude something to boast about.

Marvin, obviously determined to demonstrate how helpful he could be, rang the bell loudly and enthusiastically. Stacey hoped that Lola Smith was not startled out of too deep a sleep. Or perhaps she had taken some very potent sleeping pills—there was no sound from inside the flat.

Marvin rang another long teeth-jarring peal on the bell.

"Maybe she really *is* out," Barbara Donaldson said tentatively.

"I can't see anyone." Still keeping his fingers on the bell, Marvin applied his eye to the keyhole."

"She can't be home," Alistair said. "You're making enough racket to wake the dead."

"If she isn't there," Marvin said, "why don't we go in and look around?"

Stacey began to suspect why he had been expelled from so many schools.

"Because breaking and entering is illegal in this country," Alistair explained. "In fact, I'm sure that it's frowned upon in your country, too—What are you doing?"

"Nothing, Al." While the others had been talking, Marvin had pulled something from his pocket and scrabbled it in the keyhole.

"But, look, Al." He pushed innocently at the door and it swung ajar. "The door isn't locked. So why can't we just take a quick look inside?"

"How did you do that?"

"Do what?" Marvin backed away, almost accidently backing into the flat. "I have an enquiring mind. Everybody says so."

"I'll bet that's not all they say," Alistair said, but the open door was exerting a pull of its own. He stared over Marvin's head into the dark hallway.

"If anybody was in there, we'd know it by now," Barbara pointed out. "I don't see that it can do any real harm if we just take a tiny peek inside. Since nobody is here, Stacey can come in too, instead of waiting outside. Maybe we could find the hat-box and switch them without anyone ever being the wiser. It would sure save a lot of trouble and explanations.''

"Sure it would,'' Marvin said encouragingly. "That's what I've been telling you.'' He edged farther into the hallway. No one made a move to stop him.

Hortense, seeing Marvin unreproved, moved forward to join him. The adults hovered in the doorway, indecisive.

"Well, shoot!'' Barbara Donaldson crossed the threshold. "As well be hung for a sheep as a lamb. Come on, you two, and we can close the door behind us. Somebody might start noticing if you stand there dithering any longer.''

"I don't know how we'll ever explain this if she returns while we're still here,'' Alistair said unhappily as the door closed behind them.

Stacey agreed silently. There was a terrible finality about the way the door clicked shut. It would be awfully hard to explain just how five people had happened to wander into a deserted flat. Innocently.

"You'll think of something, Al,'' Marvin said. Happy, now that he had his own way, Marvin walked boldly down the hallway.

"That's a vote of confidence I could do without,'' Alistair muttered, following him.

The long spacious reception room faced out over the garden square. The walls were hung with heavy Chinese brocade draperies. Benares brass trays were dotted about the room standing ready to receive drinks beside deep luxuriant armchairs.

"Miss Smith does very well for herself,'' Alistair observed.

"She probably shares it with several other stewardesses." Barbara looked around appraisingly. "This sort of place would be too expensive for her to swing alone. They're rarely all in the same place at the same time, so they combine their loot and make a comfortable nest for themselves. That's usually the way it is."

"Anyway, there's no hat-box in this room." Stacey refused to be sidetracked by trivia. Lola Smith's living arrangements were the least of her worries.

"It will probably be in her bedroom," Barbara said. "But which one is hers?"

"Why don't we each choose a room and search it?" Marvin offered brightly.

"I suppose that makes sense," Alistair said. "But I still don't like it."

"None of us likes it," Barbara Donaldson said. Quite untruthful, Stacey suspected. Barbara's eyes were shining and the bored look she had worn on the plane had disappeared. Marvin and Hortense were positively revelling in the situation. It was only herself and Alistair who were genuinely reluctant. But she couldn't afford to be squeamish—she had the most at stake.

"Hortense, you'd better go with Marvin." Alistair, too, bowed to the inevitable. "Don't disturb anything more than you must. We don't want to leave any evidence that we've been here."

"Sure, Al. Leave it to me." Marvin sauntered across the room to the farthest doorway. "Stay behind me, Hortense," he said unnecessarily.

Barbara Donaldson turned and plunged into the nearest room.

Stacey and Alistair remained looking at each other for a moment then, with a shrug, Alistair muttered, "Let's get this over with," and disappeared into another room.

With a shrug of her own, Stacey turned and went through the only other possible doorway. It was a bedroom, but a preponderance of frills and ruffles somehow gave rise to doubt that it belonged to Lola Smith. Grimly, nevertheless, Stacey began working her way through it systematically.

A towering wardrobe against one wall contained a fine selection of evening gowns, cocktail dresses and attendant accessories. She looked into several shoebags hanging from the rack, but they contained nothing but shoes. Boxes with contents cocooned in tissue paper turned out to hold nothing more incriminating than matching handbags, scarves, fur stoles and flagons of unopened French perfumes.

As some of the costumes positively cried out for jewellery, Stacey began to wonder if there were a wall safe concealed somewhere in the flat.

Not in this room, however. There was no false back to the wardrobe, no pictures hanging on the walls, no place where such a safe might be concealed.

Nor was there any luggage—empty or otherwise—anywhere in the room. Stacey began to wonder how the others were doing. Especially the person who had drawn Lola Smith's room.

Back in the reception room, she met Barbara shaking her head.

"Nothing in the room I searched," Barbara reported. "But then, I don't think it belonged to Miss Smith."

But tacit consent, they drifted towards the room Alistair had disappeared into. They nearly collided with him in the doorway.

"Nothing," he said. "At least, no hat-box."

"The children—" Barbara said, with the healthy suspicion of one who had raised several of her own—"are being awfully quiet in there."

"With luck—" Alistair's thought was a triumph of hope over experience—"that's because they're concentrating on not making any mess."

But they *were* children. Marvin's precociousness and swaggering assault on adolescence had threatened to obscure the fact. As had Hortense's preternaturally Gallic sophistication, obviously an imitation of some acutely-observed female adult, possibly her diplomatic hostess mother.

They clung together in the center of the room, frozen with horror and an inability to encompass the sight before them.

"You wait outside, Hortense." Abruptly aware of reinforcements hovering in the doorway, Marvin tried to push Hortense away from him.

"*Non!*" She continued to cling. "I stay with you." Then, seeing the others had arrived, she let go and moved toward them.

"Over there—" Looking faintly green, Marvin gestured toward the bed. "We looked through the closets real good and all around the room. And then I noticed a sort of big lump under the bedspread. I thought maybe she might have put the hat-box on the bed and thrown the spread over it to sort of hide it, so I pulled the spread back and—'' He went a deeper shade of green.

"Don't you dare be sick here!" Barbara Donaldson clapped her hand over his mouth. "You know we can't leave any evidence behind. Especially now!"

The late Lola Smith lay sprawled across the bed, her face cyanosed, her eyes popping. Embedded deeply in her neck was something pale brown that resembled a nylon rope until it divided into a pair of unmistakable feet.

"She's been strangled with her own tights," Alistair said, ignoring the fact that she was still wearing her own tights.

"One of her own spare pairs, or somebody else's," Barbara corrected. "With all those girls living here, there'll be plenty of pairs of tights around."

"I'm okay now." Marvin pushed Barbara's hand away. "Al, she's dead, isn't she?"

"I'm no expert in these matters," Alistair said. "But yes, I'd say she was dead and," he added grimly, "it wasn't suicide."

"Maybe the murderer is still around." The prospect seemed to cheer Marvin. He surveyed the room with fresh interest.

"Not with the way we've been going through the place." Alistair seemed to steel himself, then took a quick step forward and touched the dead girl's wrist. "She's still warm," he reported, looking nearly as green as Marvin had been. "It can't have happened all that long ago. Whoever did it can't have got far away."

"The plane hasn't landed all that long ago," Stacey

said faintly. Already it seemed as though she'd been here for years, but she forced herself to think clearly. "It takes a long time for a body to get really cold, and she's still wearing her uniform. So she hadn't been home long when it happened. Perhaps someone was waiting for her as she entered the flat."

"Presumably carrying your hat-box," Alistair said grimly. "Which isn't here now, so the murderer made off with it. Now we really *are* in trouble."

"*I'm* in trouble," Stacey corrected firmly. "It was awfully kind of you to try to help me, but look where it's landed you. You'd better leave while you can—"

"Nuts!" Marvin said. "We're all in this together. Isn't that right, Al?"

"For once, I agree with you completely. We're in too deep now." He glanced at the body. "In over our heads."

"We ought to—" Stacey looked at the telephone beside the bed and looked away again.

"Let's get the hell out of here!" Barbara Donaldson put it into words. "If you want to do your civic duty, we can make an anonymous call from a pay phone a good safe distance away."

"Once again, I agree," Alistair said. "And the faster we get away, the better. I don't expect the murderer to return to the scene of the crime, but we can't be sure that one of the other stewardesses who shares the flat won't arrive back from Bangkok or Honolulu at any moment. It's more vital than ever that we're not discovered here."

They moved as one into the reception room. Marvin looked back in anguish. "Should we leave her there like that? Do you think I ought to put the bedspread back the way I found it?''

''I don't think we should touch anything more,'' Alistair said. He picked up the hat-box they had brought with them. ''Let's go!''

''Shouldn't we leave that here?'' Stacey asked. ''It belonged to her.''

''It's evidence that we've been here,'' Barbara pointed out. ''We don't want to leave anything behind.''

''But no one would know it hadn't been here when she was—''

''The murderer would,'' Marvin had regained his cheerfulness.

''A happy thought, Marvin, as so many of yours are. However—'' Alistair approached the door gingerly—''what I had in mind was that the hat-box was covered with our fingerprints. We don't have time to polish it—apart from which, it would be rather pointed to have a shiny black case with no fingerprints on it at all.''

''The whole flat probably has our fingerprints everywhere,'' Stacey said hopelessly. There was not much they could do about it. She could not even begin to remember all the surfaces she had touched in her search. And, as for the children . . .

''Quite right,'' Alistair said. ''But among many others. With several hostesses sharing, entertaining visitors and all that, there are probably too many layers of blurred fingerprints for any individual ones to be sorted out. The hat-box she had supposedly carried straight from the airport would be something else again.''

Nevertheless, he carefully wrapped a handkerchief around his hand before turning the doorknob.

"Apart from which," he added. "I'd rather like to hang on to that brandy. I could use some as soon as we're away from here."

CHAPTER 9

THEY PAUSED IN THEIR FLIGHT AT A PUBLIC TELEPHONE-box where Alistair made the brief anonymous call, using a foreign accent and a high-pitched indeterminate voice. Then they walked rapidly for a long distance before deciding they were far enough from the scene of the crime to risk taking a taxi.

They dropped Barbara at her hotel. She parted from them with some reluctance, but admitted she had to wait in her room for a telephone call from her husband later that evening. As she so tersely put it, "The fat will really be in the fire if Dan can't get through to me. His next call would be to Scotland Yard. He doesn't mess around."

Shuddering faintly at the thought, they had said their goodbyes in front of the hotel and driven on to the next stop: Stacey's own hotel.

"Look—" Alistair got out of the taxi behind her, the children scrambling after him. "Why don't we come up with you while you freshen up, and then you come and have dinner with us?'' He paid the taxi-driver while he was speaking and the taxi drove away. Marvin and Hortense started through the revolving door into the hotel as though the answer had already been in the affirmative.

''Come on—'' Alistair charged after them. ''We can't lose sight of those little bleeders or they'll have the place torn apart before we know it.'' He plunged through the revolving door in pursuit, leaving her alone in the entrance, debating a question which had ceased to exist.

With a sigh, she turned and followed them. After all, she might as well have dinner with them; she was not so anxious to be on her own with the problems looming over her. They waited, more or less patiently, for her at the bank of elevators.

''Well, hello there—'' The voice hailed her midway across the lobby.

With deep dismay, she saw Professor Cabot approaching, hand outstretched and beaming. There was nothing for it but to shake hands with him and try to smile herself.

''My own hotel turned out to be terrible,'' he said. ''Even though they were expecting me, they hadn't a room ready. Rather than hang around a couple of hours waiting, I cancelled and came here. I'll confess I remembered you were staying here and I thought maybe we could pick up on that drink and maybe dinner.''

''I'm afraid I can't right now.'' A distraught glance across the lobby revealed the children being bundled into the lift by Alistair. Impatience had won. Or possibly a reluctance to have it made obvious that they had joined forces. (Who, after all, *was* the Professor? They had only his word for it that he was who he said he was. It swept over her for the first time just how trusting the world was. Someone said to you, "Hi, I'm Mary Jones," and you accepted it; you didn't ask for proof, but how did you *know* it was really Mary Jones and not someone entirely different using that name for her own purpose?)

"That's too bad," he said. Stacey became aware that the Professor was looking at her rather oddly. As though he might be having a few mental reservations of his own.

"You know—and I hope you don't mind my saying this—it isn't really a good idea for you to go carrying all that around with you." He glanced meaningly at the hat-box. "Why don't you put it in the hotel safe? You'd feel a lot more relaxed." He smiled. "You might even entertain second thoughts about my offer if you hadn't that worry hanging over you."

"No, it's all right." Stacey tightened her grip on the hat-box, thankful that the Professor couldn't see the second thoughts she was actually having about him. Why had he pursued her here? Why was he being so insistent on her dining with him?

"I'm terribly tired." She smiled up at him. "Jet-lagged to the *n*th degree. I'm afraid I just want to go to my room and rest."

He knew, of course—or thought he did—what she carried in the hat-box. Thanks to dear little Hortense, everyone in the first-class cabin knew. And she wouldn't be particularly surprised to learn that rumors had percolated back to the teeming economy class compartment, as well. One air hostess would confide in another when something exciting happened to break the monotony of a long flight. The hostesses would then discuss it among themselves, gossiping in the galley, separated from the passengers only by curtains. Oh yes, the news could get around swiftly enough.

"I'm sorry to hear that," he said. "But it still doesn't invalidate my advice. You really should have that stuff locked up in the hotel safe. You shouldn't keep it with you. It's dangerous to carry it around like that."

Was he warning her? If so, he was too late. Did he realize that—was this some sort of elaborate double bluff? Perhaps he assumed that she had not yet opened the case, since she was still carrying it around with her. He might think that, if he could persuade her to deposit it in the hotel safe without opening it, the blame could then be foisted on the hotel when she eventually discovered that she had the wrong case.

Or was he genuinely the friendly adviser he was trying to appear? Was she seeing enemies where none existed when, all too obviously, she had missed noticing the actual enemy?

"You may be right," she said, turning away. "I'll see about it later. There are a few other items in my room I want to deposit with it."

"Oh, but—"

"Yes?" She half-turned, with a discouraging lift of an eyebrow. She hadn't expected her answer to be satisfactory to him.

"Nothing." He surrendered with a rueful smile. "Maybe we can get together at breakfast?"

"I was planning to have breakfast in my room," she said truthfully. "If I bother with it at all. I may just sleep straight through—'' She stifled a yawn. ''The way I feel now.''

Before he could say more, she moved away.

Alistair and the children were waiting outside her room.

''Trouble?'' Alistair asked as she hurried down the corridor to them.

''Not really.'' She rummaged for her key. ''At least, I don't think so. Just a compatriot trying to be friendly.'' She found the key and inserted it in the lock. It moved stiffly.

''Friendly, eh?'' It was impossible to tell whether Alistair was suspicious or, perhaps, jealous.

''Some people are!'' She hadn't meant to snap, but it had been an endless night and now it looked as though the day were going on forever.

''Granted. But you're not really in a position to take people on trust right now, are you?'' He added grimly, ''None of us is.''

The lock yielded and Stacey swung the door open. They crowded in behind her as though pushed by a sudden intimation that the corridor was no longer safe. They looked around and Marvin was the first to speak.

''Jeez!'' he said in awe. ''What a mess!''

''Friendly, eh?'' Alistair repeated. ''I dare say *you* didn't leave the room in this condition?''

''No,'' Stacey said faintly. ''I've never claimed to be the neatest person in the world, but this—'' She broke off and looked around incredulously.

Her suitcases had been opened on the bed and their contents strewn across the bed and on to the floor. The dresser drawers had been yanked open and left gaping. The doors to the closet and bathroom swung open. In the bathroom, the medicine cabinet had been inspected and the porcelain top of the cistern was askew as though someone had even searched the tank.

"Thorough," Alistair said. "Very thorough. I can remember that little trick from the spy film I had a bit part in, but *they* were hunting for a roll of microfilm. Surely our lot didn't think you were going to dunk that tiara in the cistern!"

"Spies, Al?" Marvin was instantly alert. "Do you really think they're spies?"

"No, Marvin, I don't," Alistair said with exaggerated patience. "I think they're just ordinary, garden-variety jewel thieves. Who aren't doing too well at the moment," he added to Stacey, "if they think *you* still have the jewels."

"You needn't rub it in," Stacey said. "In fact, I'm no brighter than your would-be jewel thief." The vision of Professor Cabot, lurking in the hotel lobby awaiting her return, rose suddenly in her mind. She saw again his eyes lingering hungrily on her hat-box, heard again his insistence that it ought to be deposited in the hotel safe.

Why? To protect her? Or to give him easy access to it? Had he already made arrangements with a confederate in the hotel to spirit away the hat-box once it had been deposited?

If he had, he'd be in for a shock when he opened it.

"Miss Orpington—?"

"Stacey," she said automatically. What was the point in being formal, or conceding to the universal fiction of prefacing her name with "Aunt?" She smiled down at the child. "What is it, Hortense?"

"This—" Hortense held out a plain white envelope. "I found it by the door. It has your name on it, *n'est-ce-pas*?" She gave the little Gallic shrug, disparaging her command of written English, as well as any consequences her find might have.

Miss E.E. Orpington. Stacey felt a chill as she glanced down at the envelope in her hand. So much correspondence from the Organizers of the Duvanov Exhibition had been addressed in just that way.

"Yes, Hortense," she admitted reluctantly. "It's addressed to me." With some trepidation, she tore the envelope open. A stiff white card fell out.

"Eustace Orpington-Blaine called. Please telephone as soon as possible." On the obverse of the card was engraved his name, address and telephone number.

"Interesting," Alistair mused, reading over her shoulder. "The question is—" he gestured at the ransacked room—"did he leave his calling card in more ways than one?"

"Who's Eustace Orpington-Blaine?" Marvin went to the heart of the matter. "Is he a relative of yours?"

"I . . . I don't know," Stacey faltered. "He sounds as though he might be." The similarity of the names was unmistakable. Was it possible that Great-Grand-Aunt Eustacia had left more behind her than she had admitted when she fled the Orpington bed and board? Had she, as lawyers so quaintly termed it, "had issue?" Was that, perhaps, the real reason there had been no serious pursuit of her, no determined attempt to force her to relinquish the Orpington jewels? Because she had left behind—traded for them—the one jewel a proud family cared most about?

"*These are my jewels.*" Cornelia had said, embracing her Gracci sons. But Great-Grand-Aunt Eustacia had never been the sentimental type. Had she considered the hard, bright, undying flames of the Orpington jewels a satisfactory exchange for a flesh-and-blood, puling, wailing child? A child, furthermore, which must have been female, since the title had subsequently devolved on a remote male cousin.

From what she knew of Great-Grand-Aunt Eustacia, it was entirely possible.

"And what do you suppose this long-lost relative of yours wants?" Alistair asked softly.

"The Orpington Bequest." The answer was self-evident. "Or at least a sight of it." Perhaps more. The current generation of Orpingtons might feel short-changed by an arrangement their forebears had considered equable. Especially in view of the price their lost legacy might fetch today.

"And isn't it unfortunate that that's the one thing you are unable to provide?" Alistair surveyed the room grimly. "Or had he already discovered that?"

"He'd only know it wasn't in the room when he searched it. If he'd seen me walk through the lobby just now, carrying the hat-box . . ." Her voice faltered.

"Maybe he'll come back," Marvin suggested cheerfully. "He might be outside the door right now."

Instinctively they all glanced toward the door.

Hortense tugged at Stacey's hand. "Let's get the hell

out of here," she said in fairly accurate imitation of Barbara Donaldson.

"Out of the mouths of babes and sucklings . . ." Alistair caught Hortense's furious eyes. "Sorry, Hortense," he said. "You're right, but I think we ought to tidy the place before we leave. The chambermaid might think the method of packing slightly unusual—even for an American."

CHAPTER 10

IT WAS NOT UNTIL THEY WERE BACK IN THE FLAT belonging to Marvin's parents, just off Sloane Square, that Stacey felt able to draw a comfortable breath. Marvin watched them sink into armchairs with a proprietorial air. He obviously considered himself their host. It was possible that despite his swaggering assurances that he would be perfectly all right on his own, he was just as pleased not to be taken at his word. Certainly, he was being excessively cordial.

"Let me get you a drink," he said. "I know where my father keeps the key to the liquor cabinet."

And if he didn't, he could open it anyway. Just for a fleeting moment Stacey remembered the ease with which he had gained across to Lola Smith's flat—and the curious stiffness of her own key in the lock of the hotel room. There had been time, while Professor Cabot delayed her in the lobby, for them to have entered her room and conducted the obviously-hurried search.

But why should they have bothered? No one was better aware that the jewels were no longer in her possession. She dismissed the random suspicion, but could not rid herself of a persistent uneasiness.

"We'll spare your father's stocks and make do with the brandy," Alistair said. "I think someone owes us that for all the trouble they've put us to. I wouldn't say no to anything you might find in the fridge, though. None of us would. It's been a long time since the last meal."

The last meal had been served by Lola Smith. That, too, was a train of thought Stacey did not wish to pursue. She got up abruptly.

"Perhaps I can be of some help." She followed Marvin to the kitchen.

"There's the deep freeze," he said, pointing. "We always keep lots of stuff in it."

A true statement, Stacey discovered, lifting the lid. Foil wrapped parcels with neat stick-on labels were stacked tidily up to the lid.

"There's a microwave oven over there—" Marvin pointed in the opposite direction. "We can get something fast."

"Just as well." Alistair had followed them out to the kitchen along with Hortense. "Where are the glasses? And the plates and cutlery? Hortense and I might as well make ourselves useful setting the table."

Hortense seemed to have other ideas. She stood on

tiptoe to rummage through the deep freeze chest with almost professional interest.

"Ratatouille," she read out, shifting a foil parcel. "Bolognese Sauce—" She tossed that parcel aside contemptuously. "Ah! Coq au Vin!" She lifted that one out.

"There's only enough for one there," Stacey protested. "Why not choose something we can all have?"

"*Non*!" Hortense clutched the parcel to her. "I will have this one!"

"It's okay," Marvin said generously. "She can have that, if she wants it. It's probably a leftover my mother put in to have by herself for lunch one day. We can all choose something different," he added with an expansive gesture. "No problem."

"I want *this*!" Hortense continued to clutch the parcel.

"Have it, then." Alistair leaned over the chest and inspected the offerings. "Why don't the rest of us have—?"

Hortense gave a scream of fury and burst into tears.

Alistair dropped the package he had been looking at and whirled around.

Hortense had unwrapped the foil and was holding a glittering jumble of gold, diamonds and lesser stones.

For a blinding moment, Stacey thought they had retrieved the Orpington Bequest, then realized that she recognized none of the pieces reflected in the shimmering silver foil. They were all strange to her—and modern.

"Aw, shit!" Marvin said. "Those are my mother's. She hides them in the deep freeze," he explained, "so any burglars won't find them."

"She didn't reckon on Hortense," Alistair said. "That

girl has a positive Midas touch when it comes to jewellery. Everything she opens turns out to be full of jewellery and worth a fortune.''

"But I wanted coq au vin!" Hortense sobbed, as stricken as the legendary Midas when he began to discover the drawbacks to his unique gift.

"I'm sorry, Hortense," Marvin apologized. "She usually labels them Hollandaise Sauce, so nobody looking for food will open it accidentally. She must've been in a hurry this time and re-used some old foil."

The foil did look as though it had seen double service. Hortense squashed the edges together petulantly and thrust it at Marvin. "I don't want *this*!" she said.

"Wait another ten years," Alistair advised. "You'll be amazed at the way your tastes have changed."

Marvin smoothed the parcel and restored it to the freezer. "How about some Chicken Maryland?" he offered, surfacing with a large foil parcel. "And maybe some corn-on-the-cob and French fries?" He dived back into the deep freeze and shuffled the myriad packages, managing, Stacey noticed, to bury the one labelled "Coq au Vin" well toward the bottom.

"I don't care," Hortense sniffed, backing away and dissociating herself from the proceedings.

"That sounds fine," Alistair said. "Why don't we leave you and Hortense to get on with it? Stacey and I will go and have our apéritif while you two cope."

Blandly ignoring Marvin's suspicious gaze, Alistair drew Stacey after him back to the reception room. He took two miniatures of brandy from one of the cartons, opened them, poured them into the glasses he had found and pitched the empty miniatures into the wastebasket.

"See here," he said abruptly. "I don't like this at all."

"I suppose you think *I* do?"

"No, I mean—" He made a gesture indicating the general unsatisfactoriness of life, particularly in recent hours. "I mean, I think we ought to telephone Barbara. Just to make sure—"

Stacey was already at the telephone. As soon as he had put it into words, she had recognized the fear nagging at her consciousness. "Do you have the number?"

"I filched a piece of the letterhead. Here." He handed it to her and stood by while she dialled and asked for the room number.

"Hello?" The voice was curiously subdued and guarded, relaxing into warmth only when Stacey identified herself.

"Oh, good. I've been wondering how to get in touch with you. Your hotel kept saying you weren't in and you didn't leave me any other number."

"What's the matter?"

"I—I'm not sure I can talk," Barbara said cautiously. "I just wanted to call and say goodbye. I've changed my mind about a stopover here. I'll be leaving first thing in the morning. I've already told Dan," she added more firmly, as though such an announcement must silence any argument. "He's expecting me. He'll be meeting my plane."

"But, Barbara, what's happened?"

"You didn't come up to my room with me. You left

me on the sidewalk outside the hotel." The voice was subtly accusing. "You didn't see the mess."

"Someone searched your room?" It was barely a question. The vision of her own violated room rose up in Stacey's mind. "Someone searched *my* hotel room, too. They must have done it while we were . . . we were in Chiswick."

"I'm sorry." Barbara's voice took on a new firmness. "I'm afraid I don't want to remember anything about that. I really can't get involved any more—" Her voice wavered. "I'm too involved already. I wish I'd never—"

"I don't blame you," Stacey said quickly. "You're right, the best thing you can do is catch that plane in the morning." She met Alistair's eyes. "If . . . if we're questioned at any time, we'll try not to let them know that you were with us."

"I'd appreciate that. I'm sorry. It's not that I'm unsympathetic, you know, but if I got any more mixed up in this, my husband would kill me—Oh! I didn't mean that! He wouldn't kill anyone. And besides, he's in Abu Dhabi—"

"We understand," Stacey said. "It's all right." But she was talking to a dead line. As though fearing the consequences of any further contact, Barbara had hung up.

After dinner, Hortense fell asleep on the sofa. Marvin, although yawning frequently, turned on the television set and maintained a pretense of deep interest in a program which could not possibly have engaged his genuine ttention for five minutes. It provided, however, an xcuse for him to stay up a bit longer.

"I think you should stay here tonight," Alistair said bruptly to Stacey. "I don't like the idea of your going ack to that hotel. In fact, I think it would be a good idea or you to remain incommunicado for a while. I imagine here's enough room here?"

"There's plenty," Marvin answered at once. "And she an use my mother's things. I don't think she ought to go ack to that hotel, either. Everybody knows where she is here."

Stacey shivered involuntarily. "I don't much like the hought of going back there myself," she admitted.

"Then there's no problem. Marvin, perhaps you'll pportion our rooms and we can have an early night. Ve've got a lot of jet lag to sleep off. In the morning, we ught to be able to think more clearly." Alistair frowned. 'And I have the uneasy feeling that there's another roblem we ought to be thinking about right now, but I'm oo tired to make the effort."

The smell of frying bacon and the lilt of happy voices ragged Stacey back to reluctant consciousness in the norning. She dressed hurriedly and went out to the itchen.

Hortense, standing on a chair by the stove, was doing acon and eggs for herself and Marvin. They had been aving an animated conversation which broke off as Stacey entered the room.

"Good morning, Stacey," Hortense trilled. "Marvin, et me more bacon, *s'il vous plaît*."

"Not for me, thanks." Stacey dropped into a chair a the kitchen table. "I'll just have coffee and toast."

"Coming right up." Marvin was still very much th host and more expansive than ever in his new rol. Neither of the children appeared to be suffering any i effects from their traumatic discovery yesterday. "Onl instant, I'm afraid. Hortense says we'll buy some coffe beans later so we can have the proper stuff."

There was something wrong with that statement, b Stacey was not disposed to examine it too closely unt she was better fortified. She watched dully as Marvi popped bread into the toaster and poured water on th coffee powder.

"Uuhh—" Alistair came into the room, crosse unseeingly to the table and slumped into the seat opposit Stacey. It appeared that he was not in the ranks scintillating conversationalists at that hour.

She didn't mind that, but he intercepted the cup coffee intended for her, removing it from Marvin's han and drinking it himself. "I need it more than you do, he apologized.

"I doubt that," Stacey murmured, but it was n worth contesting. Marvin was already preparing a secon cup.

"*You* will have bacon and eggs, Alistair," Hortens said. It was more of an order than a question.

"I'll have anything I don't have to cook myself, Alistair agreed, snaffling a piece of toast as it passed b him.

"Hortense is a good cook," Marvin endorsed. "Sh says we don't need to touch any more from the freeze

We've made out a shopping list and she's going to make a nice big tuna fish salad for lunch. It's my favorite.''

"*Salad Niçoise*," Hortense corrected serenely. "And for dinner, we will have——"

There it was again: that feeling of stepping off a step that wasn't there. Stacey met Alistair's eyes and saw that it had disturbed him, too, but he was quicker at identifying the reason for concern.

"Look here, you two," he said. "We're not settling in for the summer, you know."

"Why not?" Marvin asked. "There's plenty of room. You needn't worry," he added, "I've got plenty of money. And I know where the emergency housekeeping funds are hidden, too."

"Labelled 'Jellied Eels,' no doubt," Alistair said. "For one thing, we've got to get Hortense to her grandmother in Paris. For another——"

"My grandmother is not in Paris," Hortense interrupted blandly. "She follows the racing of her stables. She is perhaps in Chantilly. . . perhaps in Nice . . . perhaps——"

Alistair groaned and buried his head in his hands.

"You see, Al?" Marvin darted to refill his coffee cup. "It works out fine. Her family isn't around and my family isn't around, so we can join forces. There's plenty of room here——"

"Stop saying that!" Alistair thundered.

"I don't know why you're upset." Marvin was aggrieved. "There's room for you, too. And you've sublet your flat and they weren't expecting you back so soon—you said so. You could stay here with us. And so can Stacey," he said generously.

"*Enfin*, it is settled." Hortense expertly filled a plat and passed it to Marvin to set before Alistair. "Marvi and I have discussed it while you both slept. The arrange ments could not be more satisfactory."

"Oh yes they could!" Alistair stared down at his plat helplessly, as though seeking a solution there. Absently he picked up knife and fork and began to eat.

"Now really, Hortense." Stacey took up the challenge "You know it's impossible. Your family will be expectin you."

"*Non!*" Hortense shook her head vehemently. "The will not know. Grandmother will think I am with Tant Bettine, Tante Bettine will think I am with Tante Domi nique, Tante Dominique will be certain I am with grand mother. And Grandmother will be too busy with he racing to worry. And Tante Bettine and Tante Dominiqu are always so busy they barely have time to speak to eacl other if they chance to meet." She sighed wistfully. "M aunts have such pretty names. But, you see, the summe will be over and I can be back in school before anyon knows where I am."

"The terrible thing is that she's probably right," Stacey said. "Of course, that doesn't alter—"

"I hope I'm offered the part of King Herod som day," Alistair said thoughtfully. "I'm beginning to fee it's a role I could really do justice to."

"I don't know why you're worrying about Hortense," Marvin said. "*She* isn't the one who's had all he jewellery stolen and can't go back to her hotel."

"I can't go back to Thringsby either—" Stacey fel her eyes brim with tears. "I can't even leave the countr without those jewels." She turned to Alistair. "Maybe we *ought* to call in the police. We've done as much as we can by ourselves."

"Unfortunately," Alistair reminded her, "there's the little matter of the late Miss Smith to consider. The police are rather good at putting two and two together—it's their job. We might find ourselves with some very searching questions to face. About being on that plane, about a certain anonymous telephone call, about—"

"We'll deny everything," Marvin said promptly. "Nobody can prove a thing."

"Of course," Alistair said, "there *is* one bright spot: the police would immediately take the children into care. We'd be deemed most unsuitable to be in charge of them and they'd be off our hands. For good."

Marvin had started to open his mouth. He closed it again and stood silent for once. Hortense clambered down from her chair and went to stand beside him. He put a protective arm across her shoulders. They watched the adults warily.

"Then what are we to do?" Stacey asked.

"There's one last chance," Alistair said into the silence. "Your room was searched while we were gone, so was Barbara's. I've been thinking about that and, as I see it, it means that *they* don't have the jewels. They're still looking for them."

"But Miss Smith was killed—"

"Possibly for nothing. Possibly for some other reason quite outside our particular problem. When they took her hat-box away and opened it, whatever they found in it wasn't what they expected. She had the wrong hat-box too."

"It *was* a dreadful mix-up," Stacey said. "Those hat-boxes were rolling all over the place. Yet it's strange the way we were each so sure we had our own in the end."

"And how wrong you all were. Almost as if—' Alistair broke off.

"As if . . . what?"

"Just a passing thought." He shook his head groggily "As if someone were playing a game of Find-the-Lady with us. It's a card game," he explained. "Three piles o. cards, with the Queen at the bottom of one pile. The gambler shuffles the piles around and the mugs bet that they can pick which one has the Queen. They never can, o' course. But they're always certain that they never took their eyes off the right pile."

"We call it the Shell Game," Stacey said. "Only it': played with three half walnut shells and a dried pea unde one of them."

"Same principle," Alistair said absently. "The poin is, there's one more pile of cards to turn over. One las shell to lift up, if you prefer."

"Find the model," Stacey said.

"That's it. And preferably before it's too late. Some one's temper is already frayed. He's killed once; we don't want it to happen again."

CHAPTER 11

THE PARAPET OF TOWER BRIDGE WAS NOT A PLACE where one would usually have chosen to wear a silk chiffon skirt and gold tissue top while leaning out perilously into a high wind, but fashion photographs have their own sort of logic—or lack of it. Doubtless the threat to the model of either overbalancing or pneumonia was considered adequately offset by the splendid background of the grim gray Tower itself sprawled out in the field of vision.

"Personally," Alistair murmured, "I'd insist the shot be superimposed if it were me."

"That's why she gets hundreds of dollars an hour and you're still out of work, Al," Marvin explained helpfully.

"I haven't had a chance to look for work yet with you two hanging around my neck." It was obviously a touchy subject. "In any case, I don't work as a stunt man. I'm an actor."

"If she falls," Hortense whimpered, "how will we get Stacey's hat-box back?"

"We aren't sure she has it." Stacey thought it best to sound a note of caution, as much to keep her own hopes from rising too high as to discourage the others. She

shifted the hat-box she was carrying. It was the late Miss
Smith's, but considerably lighter and more respectable.
Marvin had taken charge of the sugar packets, Alistair
had removed all the brandy miniatures and the extra
cartons of cigarettes. At the last moment, she herself had
removed the notes and stowed them in her handbag.
There remained just the permitted two cartons of cigarettes and a few silk scarves.

It was now reasonable to use the pretext that they had
found it in with their own luggage and thought possibly,
from the colorful scarves, that it was the property of the
model. And please may I have my own hat-box back?
Always providing, of course, that it was in Imelda's
possession.

Fitful sunlight sparkled on the Thames and the Tower
Embankment was crowded with cheerful holiday-makers
who were, at the moment, dividing their attention between the parapet of Tower Bridge and that portion of the
Thames immediately below it. It was clear that some of
them expected more sensational developments at any
instant.

"*Do* you think she'll fall in, Al?" Marvin asked as the
model leaned farther over the railing.

"It's only too possible," Alistair said. "But, if there
were any justice, the photographer would."

"Why do we wait here?" Hortense was growing
restive. "Why do we not go up and speak to her?"

"We wouldn't be allowed to," Alistair said. "They've
had to get special permission to film there. No unauthorized
person can get past the guard. We'll have to wait until
they come down. It shouldn't be long now. They have

more filming to do at St. Katherine's Dock and they'll
want to try to get it done while the weather holds.''

He spoke with authority, having been the one who had
telephoned the Agency and obtained the day's shooting
schedule, purporting to be a harassed recently-hired exec-
utive from the advertising agency with last-minute changes
the client had insisted on having incorporated in the
script. He had been most convincing. It was quite possible, Stacey had decided, that he was a very good actor
indeed.

As though on cue, a bright flutter caught her eye. A
chiffon scarf drifted from the parapet down toward the
shimmering surface of the river, whirling erratically as it
was caught by sudden gusts of wind.

There was a flurry of activity on the bank as the second
camera crew maneuvered to keep the scarf in focus.
While the camera tracked it down, someone in the crowd
behind them screamed and pointed.

A body plunged from the parapet and hurtled through
the air in a swirl of colored silks. Evidently Imelda had
overbalanced in trying to snatch for the scarf as it
escaped her grasp.

Except for hurriedly swinging the camera to catch the
fall, the camera crew seemed unconcerned. They had
seen it all before; they had seen everything before.

The body splashed down into the Thames, sending a
minor tidal wave eddying toward the bank. After a
moment it surfaced and drifted woodenly on the water,
while one of the crew fished for it with a hooked pole
they had brought with them.

''Looked all right from here, Bobbie.'' One of the

crew spoke into a walkie-talkie to a colleague still on the parapet. "We shouldn't have to shoot it again."

On the parapet an interested set of spectators looked down on the scene, among them a figure in a brightly colored dress matching the one in the water.

"Right," the walkie-talkie crackled back. "Set up the next scene, then. We'll be right down." The figures on the parapet disappeared.

"It was only a dummy," Marvin said reassuringly to Hortense. He gazed speculatively from the parapet to the camera crew level with them, then shook his head. "Naw," he decided. "I'd *still* rather be a scientist."

"Perhaps *I* shall work with *le film*." Hortense was indulging in some speculations of her own. "It looks more *amusée* than the *Diplomatique*."

"I hate to disturb you two while you're working out your futures," Alistair said with exaggerated patience. "But we've got to get over to St. Katherine's Dock and nab our quarry before she gets caught up in the next scene."

"Right, Al." Marvin moved away instantly.

"Er. . ." Alistair paused and patted Hortense on the head tentatively. "If you *do* go into films as a director or producer," he said in afterthought, "I trust you'll think of Uncle Alistair when some good parts come along."

"If they are suitable," Hortense said equably. She turned and followed Marvin.

"God!" Alistair shuddered. "She probably will. She sounds just like one of them already."

He and Stacey trailed behind the children as they threaded their way through the crowds along the river walkway, past the gravity-defying statue of the boy-and-dolphin.

"*That* would make a good shot, Hortense," Marvin said with the proper deference due to a professional equal.

"*Oui*." Hortense surveyed it judiciously and nodded. "If it is not a *cliché* before I wish to use it." She walked on serenely, wrapped in her new professionalism.

"They'll be the death of me yet," Alistair said to Stacey. "If not one way, then another. Listen to them!"

"I have been." Stacey found herself smiling. "Don't you think it's kind of cute?"

"Cute!" He shuddered again. "There speaks a Deputy Curator of a small town museum. Wait until you get out into the real world and meet their adult counterparts."

"I'm in the real world now." Stacey stopped smiling. "And I must admit I'm not too enamored of it."

"Sorry." He took her arm, although the asphalt path stretched out smoothly before them. "I talk too much. Occupational hazard. Sorry."

"It's my fault." Stacey apologized in her turn and found herself leaning against him. "I'm much too sensitive right now. But I've never been in a situation like this before."

"Who among us has?" he murmured. "I'd say you're doing very well—for a beginner."

They reached the marina ahead of the television crew and just in time to mediate in a dispute between Hortense and Marvin.

"That was Aunt Barbie," Hortense insisted fiercely. "I am sure it was. I *saw* her."

"I don't know—" Marvin gestured perplexedly as Stacey and Alistair came up to them. "I wasn't looking in that direction. When I turned, there was nobody there."

"I *saw* her," Hortense said, with the air of one who would not be moved.

"But Barbara Donaldson must be half way to Abu Dhabi by now," Alistair said. "She's a common type," he placated to Hortense's tightened lips. "You could order three dozen of her from Central Casting any day and still have a few left over."

"I *saw* her."

They were saved by the arrival of the television crew. While the cameras were being set up, men moved about apparently purposelessly, but actually taking light-readings, checking camera angles and otherwise engrossed in myriad useless-seeming but actually vital tasks contingent to getting valuable commercial footage on to the reel.

Watching, they were taken by surprise when Imelda Butler came up behind them.

"Hello. I remember you from the plane. Doing some sightseeing?"

"Yeah, sort of." Marvin was the first to recover. He nudged Hortense sharply, but she continued staring as though mesmerized at the shiny black hat-box swinging carelessly from the strap over Imelda's arm.

Stacey, too, had observed it with a sinking heart. Surely, Imelda would not be carrying the hat-box around with her if it contained the jewellery. It was unthinkable that she hadn't opened it since getting off the plane, particularly as she was working and it must contain her make-up and accessories. Nevertheless, they were here and might as well carry on with the charade—it was their last option.

"Could we speak to you for a moment?" Alistair was already moving forward. "In private?"

"Sure," Imelda said casually. "I've got a few minutes while they're setting up the next shot." She looked around at the watching crowds. "Where?"

"Perhaps we could have tea somewhere—" He waved his hand vaguely in the direction of the shops and restaurants along the marina. "I'm afraid I don't know this area too well . . ."

They chose a quiet place and Marvin nudged them to a corner table. "If I sit on the outside with Hortense and we start a fight," he said, "nobody else will come near us. People hate to hear kids quarrelling in public, they get enough of it at home."

"Good thinking," Alistair approved. Imelda looked faintly puzzled.

Wise in the ways of restaurants, Marvin waited until their orders had been taken before starting his smoke-screen with Hortense. The people at the nearest table, with many a glare, finished more hurriedly than they had intended and left.

Wedged into the window seat, Imelda and Stacey eyed each other warily. With a pleasant smile, Alistair had seated himself beside Imelda, cutting off her escape route. Marvin and Hortense were beside Stacey and appeared to be about to come to blows.

The waitress hurriedly unloaded her tray and dashed away, leaving them to it.

Stacey tried to introduce the subject tactfully, but Imelda was shrewder than she had thought.

"Of course I've opened my hat-box. I've been using it all along." She looked at Stacey with renewed suspicion. "What's this all about? You're not just sightseeing. You needn't think I believed that for a minute."

Imelda would never quite believe anything. There was a look in her eyes, watching, mistrustful, which betrayed that, beautifully though she might photograph, her true character might be just a little less beautiful. In this case, however, she was perfectly right.

"All that confusion at the airport. You remember." Stacey spoke quickly, as though the words might be meaningless if she could get them out fast enough. "When the trolleys collided and the hat-boxes went flying—?"

"You don't mean you lost yours?" Imelda's eyes narrowed speculatively. "The one with all those jewels in it?"

"Well . . ." For an instant Stacey's mind groped frantically for a suitable evasion, even as she recognized the uselessness of it. Imelda was not going to believe anything but the truth. Nothing else would explain why they had bothered to chase her down when she was out on a modelling assignment.

"Well . . . yes," she admitted.

"And you think—" Imelda's eyes grew cold—"that *I* might have them?"

"It was just a possibility." Stacey felt herself to be on the defensive. "One of the possibilities."

"Another possibility—" Alistair interrupted smoothly—

"is that you might have noticed something we didn't notice. We were rather immediately involved in the situation—"

"Yes," Imelda said thoughtfully. "I'd have been a nervous wreck if I'd been responsible for something that valuable."

"I *was*," Stacey confessed. "I *am*. Especially," she added disconsolately, "now that I've gone and lost them. And, of course, they weren't insured at all—"

"Not insured? You're kidding," Imelda said incredulously.

"We couldn't afford it," Stacey said defensively. "Not many museums can."

"That's right," Alistair spoke as though it had never occurred to him before. "I remember when the Rembrandts were stolen from Dulwich. *They* weren't insured, either. There've been several cases in the past decade or two. All over the world. I suppose, when you think of the value of any collection of a reasonable size or importance—"

"It would cost about a million dollars a minute to insure it," Imelda finished for him. She seemed to slip into some private speculation. "You're sure they've been lost—" she asked Stacey—"and not stolen?"

"We don't want to think that," Alistair said, "but the more we try to trace the other hat-boxes, the more the chance of an honest error seems to be ruled out."

"You were almost our last hope," Stacey said, adding the "almost" more in an attempt to deceive herself than to deceive Imelda. Once they had admitted that last chance was gone, where were they to turn?

Outside, the camera crew had set up their equipment and begun gesticulating wildly at Imelda.

"Time to get back to work," she said absently. "They're ready for me now."

There seemed no point in trying to detain her. She had her own hat-box and had had all along.

The jewels were lost. Perhaps irretrievably.

"Look—" Imelda did not seem unduly anxious to break away. "You've thrown this at me very suddenly. I haven't had time to think. I won't have time to think—" She cast a surprisingly bitter look at her colleagues, whose gestures were becoming increasingly urgent. "Not until I've finished this session."

Outside, the director snapped something at one of his assistants and the young man broke away from the group and headed toward the tea-room.

"Let me think about it." Imelda pushed back her chair. "If I can sort of replay the scene in my head when I've got some peace and quiet, maybe I'll recall something useful."

"It would be marvelous if you could," Stacey said tonelessly. She and Alistair had discussed the vital moments endlessly. There seemed no real hope that Imelda could come up with anything new, even though she had viewed the scene from a different angle.

"Where can I reach you if I do?" Imelda brought out a diary and held her pen poised over a blank page.

The silence grew awkward.

"You don't really trust me, do you?" Imelda interpreted accurately.

"It's not that," Stacey said. "Not exactly. The problem is, I can't go back to my hotel. The Royal Arts Museum will be trying to contact me to arrange to collect the jewels—''

"And you don't have them," Imelda said. "You *are* in a spot! Here." She scribbled on the blank page, tore it out and handed it to Stacey. "You'd better check with me later. I can't promise anything, but it does seem to me that I noticed a few odd things about that whole flight. Give me some time to think everything over and maybe I'll remember what they were."

"We *do* hate to tear you away from your friends, duckie—'' The assistant came up behind her. "But Bobbie said to remind you that we *are* paying you."

"All right, I'm coming," Imelda said.

They watched her walk away. Marvin and Hortense allowed their quarrel to die. Alistair gathered up the bill and they left the restaurant.

Someone had been persuaded to unfurl the sails on one of the old Thames sailing barges in the yacht basin and Imelda had been helped aboard.

Crossing the bridge back to the Embankment, they could still see her as a splash of brilliance against sails the color of dried blood.

CHAPTER 12

A SENSE OF SOMETHING INDEFINABLY WRONG SEEMED to grip them all as they stood in front of the door to the flat. Marvin played with a key he seemed reluctant to use. Nor did any of them feel disposed to urge him to hurry.

"The lock looks funny," Marvin said. "I think somebody's been fooling around with it."

"You ought to know," Alistair said, a trifle grimly. "You're the expert."

Marvin acknowledged the dubious tribute with a nod of his head and crouched to squint through the keyhole.

"I can't see anything," he reported.

"We're going to have to go in, sooner or later," Alistair said. "Hurry up."

"But maybe they've got the place booby-trapped, Al. We ought to—"

"We ought to get it over with." Impatiently Alistair took the key from Marvin's hand and inserted it in the lock. The door swung back slowly, revealing an undisturbed hallway.

They jumped involuntarily as a sudden draught caught

the door and slammed it shut behind them. A trifle sheepishly, they moved into the reception room. Again, nothing appeared disturbed, but there was a sense of another presence having recently been there.

Hortense lifted her head and froze, like a small animal scenting danger.

The others heard it then: a *chir-ruk . . . chir-ruk . . . chir-ruk* sound coming closer and closer to them.

Hortense screamed with cold terror. It was the scream of one to whom a familiar object has suddenly become alien and menacing. They followed her terrified gaze and saw it.

From the far corner of the room, Pierrot was somersaulting slowly toward them, his inexorable progress fraught with a sense of impending doom bearing down on them, as though something dire and deadly might happen when he reached them.

"Bad Pierrot!" Regaining control of herself, Hortense darted forward and snatched up the toy. "What are you doing here frightening us all? I left you . . ." Her voice faltered and she turned to face the closed door of her bedroom. "I left you in my hat-box. Shut up in my hat-box!"

She stopped and seemed to listen to what she had just said, then still clutching Pierrot, rushed to her room and flung open the door. Her fresh screams galvanized them all into action.

"Don't *do* that, Hortense!" Alistair said, having checked that there was no dead body in sight. "That's the scream for the first act curtain when Uncle Geoffrey has been discovered hanging from the rafters by a rope around his neck. It's excessive for a torn piece of luggage." But his face was paler than it had been. He met Stacey's eyes with concern.

The hat-box lay open and despoiled in the middle of the bed, its lining ripped out and dangling by a few remaining threads. Suzette and the other toys lay in a tumbled heap beside it. Pierrot must have dropped to the floor and, unnoticed, begun his peregrinations.

"Jeez!" Marvin gulped and turned green. "The Hollandaise Sauce!" He turned and dashed for the kitchen.

"Coq au Vin," Hortense corrected, running after him.

The two of them were bending over the deep freeze when Stacey and Alistair caught up with them.

"It's all right," Marvin reported with relief, lifting his head from an intense study of the unwrapped foil parcel in his hands. "It's all here."

Hortense, practical instincts aroused at the sight of all that food, had begun rummaging through the other foil parcels in search of a suitable dinner.

"Macaroni, Ham and Cheese Casserole." She read out a label consideringly. "Do you like that, Marvin?"

"Sure, it's great," Marvin said absently, rewrapping his mother's jewellery. "There ought to be some frozen dough in there somewhere. We always have it with hot rolls."

Alistair signalled quietly to Stacey and they withdrew to the living-room, leaving the children to be soothed by the domestic task of preparing the meal.

"Council of war?" Stacey murmured.

"Why not?" Alistair replied. "It rather looks as though someone has just declared war, doesn't it?"

The image of the ravaged hat-box flickered across Stacey's mind and she shivered involuntarily. "They're still after the Orpington Bequest," she said. "But, if they don't have it already, where is it?"

"A good question," Alistair said grimly. "We've checked out all the logical possibilities. Perhaps it's time to start on the illogical."

"It's all so illogical—" Stacey choked back a laugh that threatened to slip out of control. "It has been ever since I left Thringsby. And now it's worse than ever. We don't know who or where these people are—" Abruptly she lost all desire to laugh. "But they know who we are."

"And *where* we are," Alistair said. "Do you think I haven't thought of that? Furthermore, they appear to have had no difficulty in gaining access to this flat."

There was a moment of silence as they absorbed the unpleasant realization: from having been the hunters, they had become the hunted.

"Do you think we ought to stay here?" Stacey broke the silence. "Mightn't it be safer to move to a hotel?"

"I'm not sure." Alistair weighed the question thoughtfully. "They know now that whatever they were after wasn't in Hortense's hat-box, so they may turn their attention elsewhere. On the other hand—" his gaze travelled to the hat-box Stacey had set down in the corner—"if they've kept the flat under observation, they now know that there's a second hat-box in here—and they may decide they want a look at that, too.

"In fact—" he stood abruptly and crossed the room to

retrieve the hat-box, "I think we ought to have a closer look at it ourselves."

He placed it on the sofa between them and began running his fingers over the lining. "The thing is," he said, "no one in their right minds who had been on board the plane and seen that tiara could possibly imagine that it was hidden under the lining. Not to mention all the other items."

"There's still one hat-box unaccounted for," Stacey reminded him. "Mine should have been in Lola Smith's possession, but we didn't find it in her flat."

"Precisely," Alistair said. "And it's my bet that no one else found it there, either. Or any hat-box at all. I suspect our Miss Smith, I suspect her most strongly. I think she was a clever little opportunist who, in the end, was too clever for her own good. A bit of smuggling was one thing—and I wonder what else she smuggled beside booze and cigarettes when she got the chance?"

"You *do* think she stole the jewels, don't you?"

"With or without assistance," Alistair agreed. "But more probably with. Her condition when we found her suggested that she might have tried to doublecross her associates, who not surprisingly lost patience with her. I think she stashed the jewels away—probably still in your custom-fitted hat-box—in a locker somewhere in Heathrow or on the way back from Heathrow.

"I think that what our burglars were searching for was something as small and simple as the key to that locker. In which case, ripping out the lining of Hortense's hat-box was a perfectly reasonable act. A small flat key could have been hidden easily beneath the lining. However—"

he finished probing and straightened up—"it doesn't appear to be concealed under this lining, either."

"But that was Lola Smith's own hat-box," Stacey protested.

"The first one she had to part with in order to take possession of another and begin her juggling act," Alistair said. "It was only an off-chance that it might have been in that one."

"But—" Stacey was interrupted by a shriek from the kitchen.

"Hortense burned herself on the stove," Marvin explained as the adults dashed into the room.

"She's too small to be doing all the cooking." Stacey was swamped by a wave of guilt. "I shouldn't have left her to work by herself."

"*Non! Non!* It is nothing!" At the prospect of her culinary authority being usurped, Hortense removed her burned finger from her mouth and spoke quickly. "I am quite all right."

"Stacey and I will finish up here," Alistair said firmly. "You two go into the other room and play."

The children looked at him with blank incredulity and Stacey realized that she had never seen them playing. Perhaps they didn't know how. They were both older than their years—which might explain some of the difficulties Marvin had had in his various schools.

"Well—" Alistair acknowledged that his choice of words had been inappropriate. "Go and do *something*. Just get out from underfoot for a while!"

"We'll go and think up more ways of trying to get Stacey's jewellery back," Marvin said with dignity. "Come on, Hortense." She followed him docilely from the room. They might be slightly unnerving as children, but there could be no doubt that they made excellent co-conspirators.

"We ought to be doing that ourselves," Alistair said. He peered through the glass door of the oven to check the progress of the casserole. "But I'm hoping some food will give us more strength—not to mention fresh inspiration."

"You know," Stacey said thoughtfully. "I've been wondering more and more about Professor Cabot. I'm still suspicious about the way he turned up at my hotel. He *said* he came over here as an exchange teacher..."

"Really?" Alistair frowned. "What university was he going to?"

"He didn't say." Stacey separated the frozen rolls, arranged them on a baking tray and popped them into the oven.

"To tell the truth," she confessed. "I didn't ask. I didn't want to get into conversation with him at all. He made me uneasy. He wasn't even supposed to be staying at my hotel. He transferred there from his own. In the ordinary way I wouldn't have cared much for that. But when I was carrying the Orpington Bequest..."

"Quite!" Alistair said. "I think your Professor Cabot needs looking into."

"I suppose I ought to go back to the hotel anyway," Stacey tried to talk herself out of her reluctance to take such a course of action, "and pick up at least one of my suitcases. I could do with a change of clothing."

"You look fine," Alistair said absently. "However, I

take your point. It would probably be a good idea to show yourself, even briefly. Reputable hotels tend to get nervous when their guests look as though they might have disappeared—and you're staying at a very reputable hotel. If you don't make an appearance now and again, the manager might do something rash—like notifying the police. And we wouldn't want that to happen.''

"We certainly wouldn't!'' Stacey shuddered.

"But we're going to eat first, aren't we?'' Marvin was hovering anxiously in the doorway. "Before we go out again?''

"Who said anything about we?'' Alistair snarled.

"Well, gee, you're not going to let Stacey go alone, are you?''

"I'll be all right.'' Stacey rather spoiled the effect by adding, "I think.''

"No, I'm *not* going to let Stacey go alone. I'm going with her.''

"And leave *us* here alone?''

"You can't leave the children here by themselves,'' Stacey protested. "Not with prowlers liable to come back to this apartment at any time.''

"I suppose not,'' Alistair said regretfully. "So it's all for one and one for all—whether we like it or not.''

"I like it fine,'' Marvin said brightly.

"Shut up, Marvin!'' Alistair said. "And let's eat.''

CHAPTER 13

WITH AN UNEASY SIDELONG GLANCE AT THE SHEAF OF messages protruding from the pigeonhole bearing her room number, Stacey walked past the Reception Desk to the bank of lifts. In a vague attempt at camouflage, Hortense walked hand in hand with her. They had reasoned that a woman with a child would be less noticeable to anyone watching for a woman on her own. Alistair and Marvin were loitering outside at what they had deemed, after some argument, to be an unsuspicious distance from the hotel.

The plan was that Stacey would pack and remove her most inconspicuous piece of luggage, to be checked elsewhere for a few hours, after which they would seek out Professor Cabot for a little talk.

The first part of the plan was accomplished easily, despite the fact that Hortense insisted on helping her pack. Since Hortense's "help" consisted of shaking out, scrutinizing and commenting upon every item in her wardrobe, the process took longer than anticipated. It was something, she decided philosophically, that, on the whole, Hortense approved of her taste.

118

Disregarding Alistair's instructions, they had shifted the bare essentials into two cases. She took the weekend case and Hortense insisted on carrying the overnight case since she had left her hat-box full of toys in Marvin's keeping. A piece of luggage obviously represented some kind of badge of importance to her.

Before leaving, Stacey took a final look around the room. A bouquet of flowers had appeared on the dressing-table since her last visit. She had assumed that they were courtesy of the hotel management but, at second glance, she noticed a small white-envelope nestling among the blooms.

She crossed over and retrieved the envelope but the telephone began to ring before she could open it. She looked up and met Hortense's anxious gaze.

"Stacey, perhaps we should leave now?"

"You're right," Stacey said. Either someone had seen them come in, or someone was trying her room periodically on the off-chance of catching her. Either way, she didn't want to know about it. "Let's get out of here."

Like birds taking sudden fright, they flew across the room and swooped on the door. Stacey was locking it behind them when she felt the hand grasp her elbow and the weekend case was firmly detached from her hand.

She turned to face a grim-visaged middle-aged man with something strangely familiar about the imperiousness of his direct gaze.

"You got my message." His eyes flicked toward the envelope she still held. "I'm glad to see you're all ready." A glance to encompass the weekend case he now held. "But—" for the first time, there was a hint of uncertainty as he looked at Hortense—"I hadn't realized you had a child."

"But—"

"Never mind." He turned on his heel and marched down the corridor, obviously never doubting that they would follow him. "We can discuss everything at home. Come along, Cousin Eustacia."

"Eustacia?" Hortense asked wonderingly. "Stacey?"

"Eustacia Evangeline." Stacey confided the worst. It was simpler to explain than the presence of this strange man who claimed her as a cousin. And yet . . . something about him reminded her so strongly of Great-Grand-Aunt Eustacia that she did not attempt, even mentally, to refute his claim. Perhaps it was his air of unconscious arrogance.

"Eustacia Evangeline," Hortense whispered, testing the syllables. "Yes, Stacey is better."

"That's what I thought," Stacey said.

"I hate my name, too." A small hand crept comfortingly into hers. "I wish my parents had not named me Hortense Hermione." She sighed. "There is not any way one can shorten either of them. Not to anything pretty."

"No." Stacey remembered Marvin's whoop of "Hor!" at the airport. "I guess there isn't."

"Come along, you two," Eustace Orpington-Blaine flung over his shoulder. "Don't dawdle!" (Shades of Great-Grand-Aunt Eustacia!)

They automatically increased speed. Cousin Eustace, it seemed, knew precisely where they were going and wished to get them there as speedily as possible. Stacey wished that she had taken the time to read his note.

They were in the lift when Hortense voiced another

problem. "But, Stacey," she said anxiously, "what about Alistair?"

"What's that?" Frowning, Eustace Orpington-Blaine turned. "Is your husband with you, as well?"

"And my brother," Hortense extemporized quickly. "Marvin." She gave Eustace her most charming smile, which he did not appear to appreciate.

"Really, this is most unsatisfactory!" he complained to Stacey. "I do think you might have let me know."

"I'm sorry," Stacey apologized ambiguously. "I didn't realize it would make a difference." What she did realize was that she was becoming as adept at duplicity as the children. Perhaps it was infectious.

"Of course it does," Eustace said. "It means another room—perhaps two. Rowena will be most put out."

"I'm sorry." Stacey felt the way she had as a little girl when the accusing eyes of the portrait of Great-Grand-Aunt Eustacia had seemed to follow her about the room. And for the same reason. Once again, she had done something to incur the Orpington displeasure.

"Perhaps," she suggested hopefully, "we could postpone this to another time?" The talk of rooms would seem to indicate a visit of some length at his home— wherever that might be. If only she could think of some excuse to get a few moments alone and read his note!

"No, no! No question of that." He was annoyed at the mere suggestion. "Rowena will simply have to cope. That's what she's there for."

"Oh." She had been thinking of Rowena as his wife, but this would seem to indicate someone of servant status. Either Rowena was just his housekeeper, or Cousin Eustace was the martinet of all time. Which, given a direct lineal descent from Great-Grand-Aunt Eustacia, was not entirely impossible.

The lift doors slid open and Cousin Eustace shouldered his way through a group of tourists, sending a couple of them flying. He did not appear to notice. With a helpless shrug to the victims, Stacey hurried across the lobby after him, trying to look as though she were not really with him but simply going in the same direction. They were followed by mutters of indignation.

Then they were through the revolving doors and out on the pavement. Eustace gave the doorman a baleful look which defied him to offer help with baggage or obtaining a taxi.

As the doorman fell back, Alistair and Marvin hurried forward, obviously fearing hijacking or kidnapping. Stacey wondered frantically how to signal them without Eustace noticing it. The whole situation had suddenly become too complicated for a simple hand or eyebrow signal.

"*Da-dee!*" Abruptly, Hortense broke free and rushed forward to meet Alistair, twining herself round him before he could say a word. "Da-dee, Cousin Eustace has come to visit us."

"And now you're coming to visit me," Eustace Orpington-Blaine confirmed, albeit still a trifle grim about it. "All of you," he added with distaste.

"Are we?" Alistair's face changed as Hortense trod on his toes heavily. "How very kind of you," he amended with a social smile.

"Yes," Eustace agreed, shaking the proffered hand

reluctantly. He eyed Marvin with suspicion. "I see you have your case ready, too. The car is this way." He turned and strode off down the street, thus missing the quick exchange of shrugs and headshakes between Stacey and Alistair.

"This is great!" Ignoring Eustace's latent hostility— he was accustomed to it from the stuffier side of the adult population—Marvin scampered forward to walk beside him. "Where do you live, Cousin Eustace?"

"In the country," Eustace said between clenched teeth. "The name of the place wouldn't mean anything to you."

"It would to me" Alistair said, drawing abreast of them.

And that was almost too much of a direct challenge, Stacey thought despairingly. How was she going to explain a French daughter, an American son and an English husband? She decided Eustace would have to supply his own explanation if he were worried about it.

"Just outside Guildford," Eustace admitted grudgingly.

"Ah yes," Alistair said. "The Yvonne Arnaud Theatre's there. Nice place."

"Perhaps you'd like to sit in the back with the children?" Eustace stopped beside an illegally-parked Rover and removed a plastic-wrapped parking ticket from the windscreen with what seemed to be an automatic gesture. "Cousin Eustacia can sit in front with me."

"Eusta—?" Alistair cut off the incredulous gurgle abruptly as Hortense bore down on his toes again.

"I'd rather sit in front," Marvin covered quickly.

"Can't I sit in front, Cousin Eustace? I want to watch you drive."

"It's not a spectator sport," Eustace reproved.

Stacey had the impression that the length of the proposed visit was dwindling by the minute. Not that it mattered. The important thing was that Cousin Eustace was unwittingly smuggling them out of the line of fire. Even a respite of one or two nights where they could not be reached or observed by unknown enemies was worth having. She felt a sudden overwhelming sense of gratitude toward him and the light-heartedness of the children told her that she was not alone. No one had been looking forward to going back to the flat; it was a failed fortress, its defenses already breached by the enemy. Even the unknown was preferable.

She slipped into the back seat next to Alistair and Hortense, aware of Eustace's displeasure as she did so. He would simply have to be displeased, however, she needed the opportunity to read the note he had sent her and she could not do that while sitting beside him.

Eustace went round to the driver's seat, slamming his door with unnecessary emphasis. "Fasten your safety-belt," he said to Marvin, carefully buckling his own.

"Okay," Marvin said, ignoring the instruction.

Eustace gunned the motor to relieve his feelings and slid the car away from the curb and out into a collision course with the oncoming traffic. Stacey had to take a deep breath and remind herself that everyone drove on the wrong side of the road over here. It was more noticeable, somehow, when one was a passenger in a car rather than just crossing the street.

"If we're so unpopular," Alistair muttered in her ear, "why does he want our company?"

"I couldn't say." Stacey began worrying the flap of the envelope, trying to open it quietly. The answer might lie inside.

By the time the car turned between two large stone gateposts and swept up a curving driveway, she was no wiser. The brief message had seemed to refer to an earlier communication, no doubt one of those piled in her pigeonhole behind the hotel's reception desk. She had passed it silently to Alistair and again there had been an exchange of shrugs. They would just have to wait and see what Cousin Eustace had in mind. It was unlikely that hospitality was his only motive.

"Here we are." Eustace halted the car in front of a large red brick building which somehow did not seem as imposing as it should be. Like Cousin Eustace himself, it just missed somewhere along the line.

"Victorian masquerading as Jacobean," Alistair muttered under his breath as Eustace came round to open the car door for Stacey.

"Shh . . ." Stacey warned as the door swung open.

A light went on behind the front windows of the house and Eustace turned toward it, abruptly and perhaps painfully reminded of something.

"I'll go on ahead," he said, dropping Stacey's hand. "Rowena won't be expecting so many. . . Er, I'll have to explain . . . I won't be a moment. If you'll just wait here, I'll come back and get your luggage out of the boot."

"Curiouser and curiouser." Alistair got out of the car and helped Hortense out. "Marvin, what are you doing?"

"Just checking the glove compartment, Al." Marvin's tone implied it was the way any sensible person would improve the shining hour. "I've been dying to get a look in it all the way down."

"Oh, is that all?" Alistair raised his eyes to heaven. "It's a start, I suppose. Just think of the medicine cabinet and all the closets you'll have waiting for you inside the house." He added hastily, "That was a joke."

"I know that, Al." Marvin's injured dignity lasted only a moment. "But it's not a bad idea."

"Look, you two," Stacey said. "Don't get carried away. This is *my* long-lost cousin. I'd rather not become *persona non grata* before we've had a chance to get to know each other. It's obviously bad enough that I should show up complete with a ready-made family."

"Yes," Alistair said thoughtfully. "He didn't like that at all, did he? I wonder why."

"Perhaps he thinks children should be seen and not heard." Stacey sent an oblique glance toward Marvin.

"I do not think I like him," Hortense said. "Are you *sure* he is your cousin?"

"He's the dead spit of Great-Grand-Aunt Eustacia," Stacey sighed. "There's nobody else he *could* be."

"Besides—" Marvin snapped shut the door of the glove compartment—"he must be." He's carrying Stacey's picture around with him."

"What?" Stacey started forward. "How could he have my picture? I've never seen him before in my life. Let me see it. It must be another cousin—one who looks like me—"

"Shhh..." Hortense was looking toward the house. "He is coming back."

"All right, all right," Eustace said. "You might as well come along now. Rowena is prepared for you." He looked at them and sighed heavily. "As prepared as she'll ever be."

CHAPTER 14

STACEY'S FIRST IMPRESSION WAS THAT ROWENA ORpington-Blaine was not prepared for much of anything the world had hurled at her, least of all living with Eustace.

"Oh!" Rowena's handshake was as limp as her hair. "I'm so pleased you could come?" She made it into a question. "All of you?" she added dubiously. Her eyes glowed with anxiety in a pale, perplexed face. She looked to Eustace for reassurance.

"Well, they're here now," Eustace said resignedly. *And there's nothing we can do about it* seemed to hang unspoken in the air.

"Oh yes. Of course?" Looking from one to another, she carelessly allowed herself to encounter Marvin's bright searching gaze. She shuddered faintly and looked away quickly. "It's just that I'm not sure where I can put you? We only have two guest rooms. And the children are a bit old to share a room . . . ?" She let the thought trail off, looking more anxious than ever.

"That's okay," Marvin said cheerfully. "I can share with Al."

"That's a very bright idea, Marvin," Alistair said through clenched teeth. "And Hortense can share with—" he glanced at Stacey—"Mom."

"Oh, if you wouldn't mind—?" Rowena's face cleared slightly. "Of course, I realize—" She stopped abruptly and her face turned crimson.

"That will be fine," Stacey said firmly.

"It will?" Rowena went even redder and abandoned any further attempt at small talk. "If you'll just follow me? I'll show you to your rooms." She turned and almost ran up the stairs.

Stacey followed at a more sedate pace, Hortense clinging to her hand again. Behind her, she heard Marvin humming under his breath, quite content with the way things were going. Equipped with a whole makeshift family, bound together by lies and larceny—not to mention being accessories after the fact in a murder—and now happily exploring a new and unknown territory, he was in his element. Military academies were never like this. If they had been, perhaps he wouldn't have been expelled from so many.

She wished suddenly, bitterly, that it were nothing but a game for her.

"Here we are." Rowena swung open a door. "You and

your little girl can have this room." She hesitated. "I'm afraid your husband's room is on the next floor up."

"That will be fine," Stacey said again. Rowena seemed to require constant reassurance.

"Yes." Rowena backed away and turned to Alistair. "I'll just show you," she said. "And then I'll leave you to freshen up? You can come down when you're ready. There's no need to change—unless you want to—we're only having high tea. I hope you don't mind?"

"Fine," Stacey and Alistair chorused together.

Rowena gave them a dubious look and turned and fled up a staircase which had abruptly shrunk to half the width of the one they had just traversed.

"I'll be right back," Alistair murmured, depositing Stacey's case just inside the door.

Stacey left the door ajar and moved into the room. Alistair had said the house was Victorian-faked Jacobean. She'd have classed this bedroom as Sears Roebuck Baronial herself.

Hortense was circling the oak four-poster with an expression every bit as dubious as Rowena's, but a lot more amused, "It is funny here," she decided. "I am glad we came, Stacey."

Another one to whom it was just a game.

"Enjoy yourself," Stacey said, "it's only a matter of life and death."

"I'm sorry." Hortense was instantly contrite and by her side. "You are not amused, that is right?"

"Very right," Stacey said bitterly. "I don't want to spoil anyone's fun, but I have a little more at stake than any of you. Like my career... my reputation... my..."

"Don't cry, Stacey," Hortense begged, agonized. "Don't cry!"

"In fact: Be of good cheer, Alistair's here!" He bounced into the room miming a fanfare.

Stacey broke off in mid-sob and looked round wildly for something to throw at him.

He dodged quickly, sensing her intention. "Now, now, let's keep the party polite. We mustn't go around breaking up other people's houses—even if they *are* your relatives."

"Hey!" Marvin whistled with admiration. "You've got a swell room. It's lots better than ours."

"So it is," Alistair said. "I think they've put us in the servants' quarters. Possibly even the tweeny's room. I haven't seen anything so cramped since I was in Provincial Rep and the entire male chorus of *The Student Prince* had to share a single dressing-room."

"I don't take up that much room, Al," Marvin protested.

"It's unlike you to be so sensitive, Marvin," Alistair said. "I wasn't complaining about the company, simply about the size of the room. It hardly makes one feel like a welcome guest, whereas this—" he looked round—"is definitely the guest-room with knobs on, if it isn't actually the master bedroom."

"I don't think it is," Stacey said. "I can't see Cousin Eustace moving out for anybody."

"No," Alistair said thoughtfully. "Not exactly the expansive host type, is he? I wonder why he was so insistent on having us."

"I should have stopped for my mail at the hotel," Stacey said. "There must have been a letter I missed. He keeps talking as though this were all pre-arranged. But I've never been in contact with him in my life—I didn't even know he existed."

"While he knew all about you," Alistair said. "Do you think he's something to do with this Exhibition of yours?"

"It's possible, I suppose." Stacey shuddered. "He could turn out to be a Trustee of the museum—he's just the type. If so, I'm in terrible trouble."

"We'll help you, Stacey," Marvin said. Hortense nodded vigorous agreement.

"It doesn't occur to you two, I suppose," Alistair said, "that you might be part of the trouble?"

"I didn't mean to—" Hortense's eyes filled with tears. "How was I to know that the plane was full of thieves? One expects this at the airport, but not aboard the plane. Not in first class."

"There's snobbery for you," Alistair said. "All right, all right, I wasn't blaming you, Hortense. I was just pointing out a fact."

"But it *was* my fault!" Hortense began to sniffle. "I was silly and stupid. And because I was, all this has happened and we . . . we are . . ."

"We're on the run," Marvin finished cheerfully for her.

"So we are," Alistair brooded. "I must say, I never thought it would be like this. I mean, it's against all tradition. Whoever heard of going on the run with two kids in tow? Alone, certainly. Or the man and woman together, yes. In *The Thirty-Nine Steps*," he added wistfully, "Madeleine Carroll and Robert Donat were even handcuffed together. That made a real sporting run." He sighed. "They don't write them like that, these days."

"They didn't then," Stacey said. "That was Hitchcock's own contribution."

"I don't believe it!"

"Go back to your source material. There wasn't a pair of handcuffs in the whole book."

"You're shattering all my illusions—" Alistair broke off to glare at Marvin. "Stop pulling at me, Marvin. If you tear my sleeve, I swear I'll make you mend it yourself."

"But, Al, Al—" Marvin clutched his sleeve more urgently—"there were lots of handcuffs on the plane, Al. There was that guy with the briefcase handcuffed to him. And there were those two guys who were handcuffed together!"

In the sudden silence, Alistair met Stacey's eyes. "He's right, you know," he said. "I'd forgotten that. I think we can most probably leave the Queen's Messenger out of our calculations but . . . those other two. Yes, it might be most interesting to find out whether that prisoner might have escaped once they left the plane at Heathrow."

"There hasn't been anything in the newspapers about it," Stacey said. "How do we find out?"

"A few judicious telephone calls should do the trick," Alistair said. "I'm afraid I wouldn't put it past your cousins to eavesdrop. We'll have to make some excuse to get to an outside phone."

There was another thoughtful silence, broken suddenly by a sharp creak from the stairs outside.

"Speaking of eavesdropping . . ." Stacey murmured.

"Yes," Alistair said. "I think it's time we went down to tea. At least, it will keep them from coming up here."

It was obvious that Hortense did not think much of Rowena's cooking. With thinly-veiled incredulity, she had dutifully eaten everything put before her but seemed about to balk at the slice of solid-textured cake now being served.

Stacey could not blame her. It looked totally unlike any cake *she* had ever seen in her life and she had a strong impression that Hortense had always moved in more rarified culinary circles. She watched, hiding her amusement, as Hortense turned the plate in a careful circle, perhaps looking for a suitable place to insert her fork or, more probably, playing for time while she thought of an excuse to avoid eating it at all.

"Don't you want your pudding, dear?" Rowena asked.

"Pudding?" Hortense's face cleared. "I thought it was cake."

"Oh, well, of course, it is. We just call it pudding because it's the sweet course, you see?"

Hortense scrutinized the cake again, as though the answer might be there to see. "This is very English, yes?"

"Oh, yes. It's an old English favorite. It's Lardy Cake."

"Yeah." Marvin poked at blob of congealed grease sparkling with sugar crystals. "It sure is."

"Oh dear!" Rowena was instantly on the defensive. "I'm afraid it didn't turn out too well—"

"It's fine," Alistair said, nobly aiming a huge forkful

into his mouth and struggling with it. He swallowed with difficulty. "Just fine. But perhaps you have to be English to appreciate it."

"That may be true." Eustace Orpington-Blaine looked at Stacey strangely before turning to the children, his teeth bared extravagantly in what was obviously intended to be a winning smile. "And you're not English, are you?" he asked Marvin.

"Heck, no!" Marvin said. "I'm American."

"And you're not?" The teeth glinted at Hortense.

"I am French," Hortense affirmed quickly. Then a sudden wariness shadowed her eyes. "Like my father," she added triumphantly. "Stacey's last husband."

Stacey choked on a piece of lardy cake which seemed to have turned to sand, despite the greasiness. But Eustace Orpington-Blaine just nodded in satisfaction, as though a private suspicion had been confirmed.

"My father was her *first* husband!" Marvin took up the challenge so quickly that it sounded as though the subject were one of long-standing contention between the children. "My father is an American," he added unnecessarily. "He's a General in the Army."

"*My* father is in the *Diplomatique*," Hortense riposted proudly.

"And . . . er . . . you?" Eustace looked to Alistair.

"I'm an actor," Alistair said.

"Hmmm." It was only too obvious that Eustace considered that Stacey had come down in the world.

"I was in a Broadway show." Now Alistair was on the defensive.

"But it didn't run, Al," Marvin reminded him.

"Thank you, Marvin," Alistair said. "If you're ever looking for a job as a public relations officer, don't come to me."

"And you haven't any . . . er . . . ?" Eustace looked from Marvin to Hortense.

"We haven't been together very long," Stacey said truthfully.

Eustace nodded and sent Stacey an oddly conspiratorial glance. Rowena plucked nervously at the tablecloth, but a knowing smile quirked the corners of her lips. Stacey began to feel extremely uncomfortable.

Hortense had taken advantage of Rowena's preoccupation with the conversation to reduce her slice of cake to a large heap of crumbs which she proceeded to push around her plate, trying to make it look as though she had eaten most of it. Stacey wished she had thought of that; she could not follow Hortense's example without giving them both away.

"By the way," Alistair said. "I'd rather like to make a couple of telephone calls. Is there a pay-phone anywhere near by?"

Eustace raised his eyebrows. "Our telephone is in my study. You're quite welcome to—"

"They're Transatlantic calls," Alistair said.

"Oh!" Eustace's eyebrows descended abruptly. Alistair's welcome had just run out. "In that case, er, perhaps the pub—"

"Splendid!" Alistair beamed with relief. "Why don't we all go along and have a drink? You'll be my guests."

"How very kind of you." Eustace rose with enthusiasm. "There's a jolly little place just a couple of miles from here. You'll like it." He nodded to Stacey. "All the Americans do. Very atmospheric."

Even Rowena had risen and was clearing the table with something approaching animation. Clearly she intended to be included in the little jaunt.

"Oh, but—" Stacey looked around dubiously. "Perhaps I ought to stay here with the children?"

"Nonsense," Eustace said. "No need for that. They can come with us."

"To a pub?"

"Yes, yes. They won't be allowed inside, of course. But you can stand outside the door." He beamed jovially at the children. "Wouldn't be surprised if there weren't other children there—it's a popular place. We'll pass you out crisps and orange juice. It's a mild night—and raining. We won't be long. You won't mind that, will you?"

"Sounds great," Marvin said.

"I would like that." Hortense was beaming too, but that may have been because Rowena had just removed her plate without making any remarks.

"Of course you would," Eustace said. "All quaint and amusin' and seein' how the other half lives, right?" He glanced at his watch.

"Plenty of time, isn't there?" Taking his cue, Alistair glanced at his own watch.

"Oh, plenty, plenty," Eustace assured him. "Just checking—telephone call I have to make myself. Want to catch the chap at home. Local call," he added pointedly. "I'll be right back."

CHAPTER 15

THE SALOON BAR OF THE DANCING HARE WAS CROWD-ed, noisy and, as advertised, determinedly quaint.

"*Mine eyes dazzle*," Alistair complained softly to Stacey, shielding them with his hand. "They've rather overdone the horse brasses, haven't they?"

"Either that or the metal polish," she agreed, blinking.

"I'll take care of the kiddiewinks," Eustace said, shouldering his way through the crowd, waving expansive greetings to his friends. "I know the ropes." He collared two large packets of crisps and pointed to the fruit juices as the landlord moved forward to greet him.

"And the rest is mine." Alistair picked up his cue. "What would you like? A cognac after that excellent tea?"

"Very nice," Eustace agreed, "Hang on, let me introduce you to the landlord. Let him know you're with me and he'll see you right. I mean, you might need extra change for the phone—that sort of thing."

Alistair duly went through the ceremonies and handed over several notes from which, Stacey noticed, despite Eustace's protestations, the entire sum was deducted.

"Phones are back there—" Eustace waved vaguely. "We'll be here by the fire." He handed Stacey the bottles of orange juice and the crisps, carrying the glasses himself. She followed him with only one anxious backward glance for Alistair, who appeared to know his way around a pub as, indeed, he should.

"Here you are—" Eustace said, opening the Saloon Bar door and allowing Stacey to distribute the refreshments to the waiting Marvin and Hortense. "If you want any more, just open the door and whistle to us. But you mustn't step over the threshold, mind, the licensing laws are very strict. You might get the landlord into trouble. We wouldn't want that, would we?"

"That's all right," Marvin said. Magnanimously, Stacey thought, in view of the smell becoming increasingly apparent in the courtyard. "We're having a very interesting time here. This is Judy—" He introduced a small girl hovering beyond the rim of light from the doorway, clutching a tin of cola and a box of cheese crackers. "Her father has just bought a truckload of chemical fertilizer for his farm. It's over there." The last remark was unnecessary. Anyone within a mile radius would have been able to pinpoint the location of the fertilizer.

"Yes, yes," Eustace choked. "Well, enjoy yourselves." He retreated hastily into the warmth and malt fragrance of the Saloon Bar.

"I'll just go and see if Alistair has got through to the States," Stacey excused herself quickly. A private conversation with Eustace and Rowena was more than she felt able to cope with at the moment. "We'll join you as soon as he's finished."

"Yes, yes." His gaze already focused beyond her on several friends who were signalling to him, Eustace had obviously lost interest in his newly-discovered relative. "Take your time. No hurry. We've an hour and more until closing." He moved off toward his cronies.

Stacey came up behind Alistair in time to hear him saying querulously, "See here, old man, I'm only doing my job. It's a reasonable question, it deserves a reasonable answer. Mean to say, we've had this tip-off and all we want is confirmation. A simple 'yes' or 'no' will suffice—"

There was a frantic gabbling from the other end of the line.

"That's all very well, but it's begging the issue," Alistair said sternly in his new role of investigative journalist. "Mean to say, you *must* know. If you don't, who does? You're Security, after all, aren't you? Well, there you are!"

The frantic gabbling increased.

"You can't tell me whether a criminal who was being extradited from the United States in handcuffs escaped after disembarking from the plane at Heathrow? You didn't even know one was coming in on that flight? Yes, of course, I'm sure. I saw—I mean, I had a friend on board and he saw them handcuffed together. And you say you don't know anything about it? What kind of records do you keep there, anyway?"

As Alistair's eyebrow's rose, Stacey leaned forward to try to hear the other end of the conversation. Their foreheads touching, he tilted the earpiece between them so that the voice became clearer, if not more definite.

"Policeman in charge . . . unnecessary. No papers anyway . . . seldom do have when they're arrested in another country and brought back. Usually very sudden. They radio ahead to warn Immigration. Then they're rushed right through, straight out to a waiting police car. Hardly anything to do with us, at all."

"You mean to say—" Alistair's voice rose incredulously— "you mean these people can come into the country without any passports?"

"Just explained, haven't I? Returned criminals . . . police aren't going to worry about letting them pack their cases or any formalities like that. Papers are superfluous when they're already in custody. The main object is to get the prisoner into a cell as fast as possible. Everything else gets sorted out later. Nothing to do with us."

"I see," Alistair said grimly. "So you don't know anything about it?"

"What I've just been saying, isn't it? Over our heads. Check with Scotland Yard. They ought to know." He rang off abruptly.

"Which is just what we can't do, of course." Alistair replaced the receiver thoughtfully.

"If there'd been as escape, wouldn't it have been in all the newspapers?"

"Not necessarily. The police might prefer to keep it quiet while they tried to recapture him. It would depend on how important the criminal was—"

"But if he was being extradited—"

"And what he was being extradited for. Some charges are more serious than others. But someone ought to know something. Someone we could safely approach." He frowned. "Do you still have that list of Miss Smith's?"

"In my handbag." Stacey began to open it. "But it didn't have all the passengers on it. I'm pretty sure she didn't have those two listed."

"Perhaps not but, as I recall, there were the names and telephone numbers of a couple of the crew. One of them might know something."

As usual, the item being searched for had slid to the deepest and farthest reaches of the handbag. Stacey rummaged for it resignedly.

"Al! *Al!*" There was the sound of pounding feet and, disregarding the indignant remarks of the regulars and the anguished cry of the landlord, Marvin raced through the Saloon Bar and skidded to a halt in front of them.

"Al! Stacey! Come quick!" He grabbed their hands and began pulling them back through the bar. "Hurry up—they've got Hortense!"

"What? Who has? What's going on here?" Eustace caught up with them as they flew through the doorway.

"I knew it wasn't safe to leave children standing around outside a bar," Stacey sobbed. "I never should have let—"

"It was my fault," Marvin accused himself. "I shoulda stayed with her. I only left her for a minute because Judy's father was coming back and they were leaving and I wanted to get a good look at that truck first. She was standing by the door—I kept an eye on her. But then that guy came back and—"

"Take it easy—" Alistair looked around the deserted courtyard. "What guy?"

"The one who'd been talking to us a few minutes ago. He was more interested in talking to the girls than to me. I shoulda known. I didn't like him at all. Hortense didn't, either, but she was polite to him."

"Oh God!" Stacey sagged weakly against Alistair. "We'll have to call the police now."

"No, we don't, Al," Marvin said. "We can go after them and get her back. I saw which way they went. They won't get far."

"They could be in the next county by now—" Alistair began.

"No, no," Eustace broke in quickly. "These roads are too narrow and winding; they won't be able to get up any speed. The boy is right. If you go after them, you might be able to catch them. If not, time enough to bring the police into it."

"Did you get the license number, Marvin?" Alistair asked.

"I couldn't read it—it was all muddy. I didn't want to clean it up and look. The guy would have noticed. Besides—" he shrugged—"I didn't think it mattered."

"Mattered!" Stacey said.

"It's all right," Marvin said. "It isn't what you're thinking. He was only talking to the girls so's he knew which one had the French accent. He didn't want to snatch the wrong one."

"Oohhh," Stacey wailed. Anyone deliberately singling out Hortense for kidnap would want only one thing for ransom—and, even if it were hers to give, she no longer had it.

"Let's get going," Marvin urged, looking pointedly at

Eustace. "Your car is better than theirs. We can catch them. If we start now."

"Yes, yes." Eustace glanced over his shoulder. "See here—" He spoke abruptly to Alistair in a man-to-man voice. "I can't leave my wife right now. She's too upset—"

"*She's* upset!" Alistair said.

"I know, I know. Sorry and all that—" Eustace fished a set of keys from his pocket. "You'll have to carry on without me. We'll hitch a ride with friends. Better that way, eh? Someone waiting back at headquarters in case they try to make contact? Here." He thrust the keys at Alistair. "You go after them. Perhaps—" his tone offered no real hope—"perhaps you'll manage to catch up with them."

"Thanks," Alistair said shortly. He wheeled and headed for the Rover, Stacey and Marvin at his heels.

Eustace stood looking after them until the car motor roared into life. Then he turned and went back to Rowena as the car shot down the driveway.

"That way, Al." Marvin pointed out the first turning. There were no street lamps and the night was dark. "They were going around fifty-sixty an hour. They won't get far."

"At that rate," Alistair swung the car into the curve, "they could be half way to London by now."

"Oh no," Marvin said with assurance. "Not more than a mile or two. And Hortense won't stick around once they've stopped." There was a trace of admiration in his voice. "She's a real smart kid—for a girl."

Alistair glanced sharply at Marvin but, as the road

narrowed abruptly, he was forced to concentrate all his attention on the winding strip of asphalt. They tires hummed, the car shook, as he pushed the speed as high as he dared.

It was unfamiliar terrain. They were hemmed in by hedgerows, unable to see beyond the next curve. There were no dwellings, no signs of life, along the way. They might have been driving on an uninhabited planet.

The road grew narrower, the hedgerows higher. At least, there was no question of an alternative route. Once they had taken that first turn, they were committed to this direction. Ploughed, sloping fields rose behind the hedgerows; they were in the heart of the Green Belt, agricultural land all around them.

"I hope you know what you're talking about," Alistair murmured, following yet another twist in the road.

"Any minute now," Marvin said. But the tension in his frame as he leaned forward trying to see into the darkness ahead belied the ease of his words.

Suddenly there was a crossroads and, just beyond them, the dark hulking shape of another car in the middle of the road.

Cursing, Alistair slammed on the brakes.

"That's it!" Marvin had the door open as the car wrenched to a stop. "That's the one!" He leaped out and disappeared into the darkness before Stacey could stop him.

"Come back here!" Alistair shouted uselessly. "Marvin!" But he was gone.

"That's torn it!" Alistair switched off the engine; the

silence of the night settled around them. "Now we've lost both of them!"

"He seemed to know what he was doing," Stacey said faintly. It was not much to offer.

"Marvin always *seems* to know what he's doing," Alistair said bleakly. "But he's only twelve years old, when all is said and done." He slumped down in the seat. "And I'm responsible for him. For both of them."

"We'd better go after them." Stacey struggled out of the car. Ahead of them, the other vehicle loomed dark and menacing. Both front doors were ajar, parking lights still glowed, but the body of the car was dark.

Stacey moved closer to it and realized that the windows were of the one-way tinted glass beloved of Pop idols, celebrities . . . and gangsters. Anyone inside could see out, but anyone trying to look in could see only blackness.

"Careful—" Alistair caught her arm and moved her to one side before cautiously approaching one of the doors. He stopped and tilted his head at a listening angle.

"Hortense?" he whispered. "Hortense, are you in there?"

No sound came from the car.

"Hortense?" Standing behind the door, he swung it open slowly.

The car was empty. Only the dimly glowing interior lights gave any sign that it had ever been occupied recently. Even as Stacey bent to look inside, one of those light bulbs flickered and went out.

"Not exactly in first-class condition," Alistair said. "Looks like a hire car."

"Then we ought to be able to find the name of the person who hired it."

"Find the name he *used*," Alistair corrected. "I can't imagine it would be his real name. Or that it would get us very much farther."

"He'll have to contact us sooner or later," Stacey said. "He's got Hortense."

"No, he hasn't," Marvin said, so loudly that they jumped. He had come up behind them while they were engrossed in the car. "I've got her!" Sure enough, the child was close behind him.

"Oh, well done, Marvin!" Alistair exclaimed.

"Hortense!" Stacey swooped on her and hugged her with relief. Hortense appeared unperturbed by her recent kidnapping. "What happened?"

"When the car stopped," Hortense explained calmly, "I got out and ran and hid in the bushes while the man was still trying to make the engine go again. It was very dark and he couldn't find me. I think he was not accustomed to the country. He kept sliding and falling. Then, when he heard your car coming, he ran away. I think he will not bother us now."

"You don't seem bothered, at any rate," Alistair said, not without admiration. "Weren't you frightened or worried at all?"

"Oh no," Hortense said. "I knew Marvin would rescue me."

"That's right." Marvin patted her shoulder awkwardly. "I'll take care of you."

"We appear to be superfluous," Alistair said to Stacey. "However, as we're still *in loco parentis*, I'd suggest we all get out of here. Just in case that character is still hanging around—perhaps with a gun. He might not use it on the kids, but I doubt if he'd have many scruples about us. He'll probably want to try to regain possession of his car.''

"I think he's given up on the car, Al," Marvin said. "If he's smart, he has. That car isn't going anywhere for a long time."

"That's right." Alistair spoke with sudden renewed suspicion. "You kept saying they weren't going to get far. How did you know?"

"Well, you see—" Marvin squirmed uncomfortably—"I didn't like that guy. I didn't like the way he was looking at Hortense. I didn't trust him. I just didn't like him."

"You've established that point, Marvin. Go on."

"Okay. So, while he was still talking to the girls, I went and sort of had a good look at his car. Just in case."

"But you didn't bother to take the license number." Alistair spoke slowly and thoughtfully. "The windows were tinted, so that you couldn't get a glimpse of the petrol gauge—which wouldn't be registering anyway without the ignition turned on. And yet you knew they couldn't get far—"

"That's right, Al." Marvin tried to change the subject. "Why don't we get going?"

"Marvin, just what *did* you do?"

"Oh...uh...well...I sort of poured some sugar in the gas tank..."

"You put sugar in the petrol tank?"

"That's right. I've got lots of those little packets of sugar from the plane—"

"Marvin—" Alistair choked. "Do you know what sugar in the petrol tank does to the engine of a car?"

"Sure, I do, Al," Marvin said with injured dignity. "That's why I got expelled from Roanoke."

CHAPTER 16

"AL," MARVIN SAID CAUTIOUSLY. "AL, I'VE BEEN thinking."

They had been driving without haste through the darkness, at times not entirely sure that they were going in the right direction, but persevering none the less. They were in no hurry. Eustace would not contact the police until they had returned to admit the failure of their mission. Since they had not failed, the police could still be kept out of it. For a while longer.

"We're not lost, Marvin," Alistair said defensively. "Just as soon as we get back on the motorway, I'll know where we are. We'll be back in the bosom of Stacey's family before you know it."

"That's what I mean, Al. I don't think it's a good idea. I don't think we ought to go back there."

The car slowed as though of its own volition. "That's very interesting, Marvin. Why not?" Alistair glanced at him suspiciously. "You haven't done anything there, have you? We're not *persona non grata* already?"

"Nothing like that, Al." For once, Marvin was too intent upon what he was saying to take umbrage. "It isn't me, it's them. There's something funny about them, didn't you notice? Especially that Eustace guy."

"He isn't exactly hail-fellow-well-met, I'll agree, but—"

"He made a telephone call just before we went out, didn't he? And then Hortense was snatched. How did they know where to find us?"

"I do not want to go back to that place," Hortense said decisively. "Marvin is right."

"I'm afraid I agree," Stacey said. "I don't trust Cousin Eustace as far as I could throw him. I'd rather not go back to that house, myself."

"That makes it unanimous." Alistair slowed the car. "I don't fancy it, either. Of course, it leaves us with a few little problems. We happen to be in possession of Eustace's car, for instance."

"They've got all our cases," Marvin pointed out.

"Hardly a fair exchange. The car is worth considerably more."

"Yeah, but do they know it?"

"Marvin, you undoubtedly have the most mistrusting attitude I have ever encountered. So far. Mind you, I expect to meet a fairly close match for you when we all try to check in at a hotel at this hour of the night and with no luggage."

"We could always sleep in the car."

"No, Marvin, there I draw the line. We may come to that, but let's leave it for a last resort. In any case, we need access to a telephone. There are more calls I want to make and I don't want to be distracted by feeding coins into a paybox. Right now, a hotel is our best bet.''

The road ahead veered sharply, dipped and flattened out to decant them into a brightly-lit, well-sign-posted roundabout which promised proximity to several large towns and eventual access to London.

"Here we go," Alistair muttered, turning into the main carriageway but heading in the opposite direction to London. "And where we stop . . ."

Nobody knows. Stacey could have done without picking up his thoughts so accurately. They were not particularly comforting thoughts. Nor, for that matter, were her own.

"How long do you think it will be before Eustace reports the theft of his car?" She voiced the one uppermost in her mind.

"It will be quite a while before he realizes we've gone missing." Alistair had obviously been giving the matter some quiet thought. "For the first few hours, he'll assume we're still chasing after Hortense and have either got lost or don't want to return and admit defeat. It will be morning before he begins to worry. Even then, he seems no more anxious to drag the police into this than we are."

"Suppose the guy calls up to tell him he's lost Hortense?"

"Even more reason not to bring the police into it. But the kidnapper might have followed us from London and not be in league with Eustace at all." A fine sleeting mist had materialized and Alistair switched on the windscreen wipers. "I vote that we drop Eustace a postcard and tell

him where he can find the car, once we've moved on.
That will demonstrate our good intentions without giving
away our whereabouts. He won't be able to complain
about that. Not unduly."

They were approaching the outskirts of a town. A
sprawling cluster of lights on one side of the road marked
a country inn with restaurant and pub.

"We might as well try here." Alistair swung the car
into the courtyard and parked in an obscure corner.

"I think," he said, as they got out of the car, "we'll
tell them that we have a long way yet to go and the
children were getting carsick, so we decided to put up for
the night. Can you manage to look carsick?"

Hortense sucked in her cheeks and looked improbably
ethereal. Marvin produced graphic retching noises.

"Forget it, Marvin!" Alistair shuddered. "Our chances
of shelter for the night won't be improved if they think
you're likely to ruin the carpet. Let's just stick with
saying that Hortense felt carsick."

They entered the lobby in time to hear a chorus of
groans from the bar as the bartender called out, "Time,
gentlemen, please."

"That's unfortunate timing." Alistair glanced at Stacey.
"Still, perhaps we won't be regarded as suspect with a
couple of children with us. You stay here while I talk to
the desk clerk."

Disregarding the suggestion, Marvin followed Alistair
across the lobby. Stacey and Hortense remained just
inside the door, grateful for the warmth. Stacey noticed
idly that Marvin had a box of cheese crackers protruding
from his jacket pocket. He must have swapped his packet

of crisps for them with the little girl back at the Dancing Hare.

Alistair appeared to be having no luck with the desk clerk. Alistair must really be quite a good actor, she decided. Even his back was eloquent, projecting supplication, explanation, indignation and, finally, dejection.

He was shaking his head as he crossed the lobby to rejoin them, but Marvin lingered at the desk, engaging the clerk in conversation.

"No luck," Alistair reported, coming up to them. "He claims they're fully booked, but I don't believe it for a minute. I'm afraid we just have to face the fact that we look suspicious." He brooded on this for a moment. "Not surprisingly, I'd say, in view of the life we've been leading lately. I used to be an honest, straightforward, unsuspicious sort of bloke, but—"

"It's okay, Al," Marvin said, coming up behind him. "It's all fixed."

"But that was before I met Marvin," Alistair finished, and did a double-take. "*What* did you say?"

"It's all fixed, Al. They've found room for us, after all."

"I'm so very sorry—" The desk clerk rushed up to them. "There's been an error. The young gentleman has explained. Of course we have room for you. If you'll just come this way, my lord." He turned toward Stacey and sketched a bow. "My lady..."

"I'd like a word with you, Marvin," Alistair said as the door closed behind the desk clerk, who had insisted on conducting them to their rooms personally. "Now that we're alone."

"What's the matter, Al?" Marvin's innocence was injured yet again. "I got us in, didn't I?"

"At what price? Or, to put it more plainly, how?"

"It was easy." Marvin shrugged. "I just said to the guy, 'Don't you know who that is? That's—' "

"Yes, Marvin?"

"Well, it wasn't a lie," Marvin defended. "It's just like, you know, at school, when they call the roll: 'Birnbaum, Marvin. I just said your name that way round, only I sort of ran it together quickly and I guess he thought I said, 'Lord Alistair.' He sure got excited."

"And so I was raised to the peerage!" Alistair sighed heavily. "Marvin, have you no scruples?"

"Well, we wanted to stay here, didn't we? It worked. And besides, if anybody comes looking for us now, they'll never recognize you by that name."

"It was a very good idea, Marvin," Hortense applauded. She was struck by a new a happy thought. "If I'm your daughter," she asked Alistair, "does that make me a Lady, too?"

"Not necessarily. An Honorable, perhaps. It depends on what degree of peerage is involved. I don't suppose you specified too closely, Marvin?"

"Gee, Al, what do you have to be like that for? I thought you'd be pleased."

"Sorry, Marvin. It's just that I'd like a bit of warning about these things. It could have been very sticky if he'd wanted me to register before he showed us to our suite.

As it is, I suppose I can just scrawl a lordly 'Alistair' in the register and let them take it from there.''

"They seem to have done us proud," Stacey said. They were in a cozy sitting-room with a bedroom opening off it on each side and a luxury bathroom and cloakroom flanking a tiny entrance hall. "Maybe you ought to pose as a peer of the realm more often."

"I may make a lifetime career of it," Alistair said. "A few more lessons from Marvin and I can get the best cell in Wormwood Scrubs."

"It's nothing illegal," Marvin protested. "You can call yourself anything you want. And it's even your real name—it's just sort of turned back to front, that's all."

"That's enough," Alistair said. "Still, you're right, and as long as I don't try to profit by it, it's not illegal. Since I shan't try to have the bill forwarded to a mythical peer, I'm safely within the law. This time. But, Marvin, I would appreciate advance warning when you're going to pull a stunt like this in the future."

"Don't be silly, Al," Marvin said. "How do I know what I'm going to do until I do it?"

Alistair shuddered. "Let's close the subject. It's time you two were in bed." He looked hopefully at Stacey. "Same arrangements as before, I suppose?"

She nodded.

"Oh well," he sighed. "It was worth a try."

"I'm not tired." Marvin put up the usual last-ditch defense.

"Nor am I." But Hortense couldn't help yawning.

"*In*!" Alistair flung out his arms, pointing in opposite

directions, like a stern Victorian patriarch hurling his progeny out into the storm.

"Can't we even watch television for a while?"

"*In!*"

"Shouldn't we do something about baths for them first?" Stacey enquired. This cleared the room without further protest.

"Probably we should," Alistair said. "But do you happen to have enough energy left to argue that particular toss?"

"No," she admitted, sinking down on the sofa.

"Neither do I." He sank down at the other end and stretched out his arm for the telephone. "I may have just enough steam left to make those telephone calls—but I'll have to force myself." He hesitated. "I assume you *do* still have the numbers?"

Stacey reached wearily into her handbag and brought out the sheet of paper they had inherited from Miss Smith. She passed them to him and watched listlessly as he battled with the operator and finally won through to a direct-dial outside line.

"At this hour—" he dialled briskly—"I suspect Friend Imelda would be our best bet, although I wouldn't like to sweat to it. By this time, she may be on the opposite side of the world modelling something exotic in Pago-Pago."

Stacey leaned back and closed her eyes while they waited for the call to be connected. The brief respite reminded her that she had been planning to spend most of this trip thinking about what she had previously, in her unknowing innocence, considered the problems of her life.

Gordon . . . She had intended to come to a decision about Gordon. But he now seemed to be such a remote part of a previous existence that she found it hard to call his features to mind. She was bitterly certain, however, that he would not have been any tower of strength if he had been with her through all this.

Alistair, on the other hand, although groggy was still game. "Lord Alistair here," he said, obviously deciding that Marvin's ploy was worth working right into the ground. "Actually, it's rather urgent. I'd appreciate it if you could put me through directly."

Stacey could hear an obsequious squawking at the other end of the line and then the click as he was connected. There was a puzzled but enthusiastic greeting from the other end.

"No, no," Alistair cleared it up quickly. "Lord is my name. "Alistair Lord—you remember? Yes, that's right . . . Really? Can't imagine where anyone could get such an idea."

The enthusiasm ebbed but, at least, Imelda had not hung up on him. Presumably she had meant it when she had offered to help them.

"We were wondering if there were any developments at your end? You were going to have a quiet think about our problem. Have you had time yet? I realize you're a busy woman, but time's getting short for us."

Time was running out. It was nice of him to say "us," but the opening date for the Exhibition was just a few days away. If the American courier did not turn up soon with the promised exhibit, how much longer would the organizers delay before setting wheels in motion? And what wheels?

At the very least, they would telephone Gordon, who would assure them that he had personally watched her board the London flight. A check with Customs at Heathrow would confirm that she had arrived safely. And then the fat would be in the fire.

How could anyone—police or museum officials—believe what had happened from that point onward?

Except—she felt a cold chill—the police would believe *something* had happened. They had Lola Smith's body to prove it. And they would be most anxious to have a long and meaningful conversation regarding the circumstances in which said body had been discovered and unreported. Well, reported anonymously—which, if anything, only made the situation worse.

The inevitable conversation with Gordon didn't bear thinking about. It was hard to decide which he would consider the more reprehensible: losing the fortune entrusted to her care, or getting involved in a messy foreign murder case. In all the annals of Thringsby—both family and town—nothing of the sort had ever happened before.

"Are you all right?" She opened her eyes to find Alistair watching her with a worried expression.

"Yes, fine." She realized that she had moaned aloud. "I was just thinking . . ."

"I don't advise it. It's a dangerous occupation at a time like this. Unless—" he added hopefully—"you've thought of something useful?"

She shook her head regretfully. "Has Imelda?" Caught

up in her own private concerns, she had lost the thread of the telephone conversation.

"Who knows?" He grimaced. "She seems to think she has, but she didn't want to discuss it over the telephone. She has people there. Some of the crew came back after the day's shooting for a few drinks. She wants us to come there in the morning and she'll tell us then. It looks as though Cousin Eustace doesn't get his car back for a while yet."

"Might as well be hanged for a sheep as a lamb," Stacey said resignedly. With all her other problems, alienating relatives she had never seen before seemed the least of them. It would not upset her greatly if Cousins Eustace and Rowena never spoke to her again; an eventuality which seemed only too likely.

"We don't hang people in this country any more. Not even for murder. Although," he added thoughtfully, "it's quite true that one is likely to get a longer sentence for theft than for murder these days."

The thought, with its attendant vision of Lola Smith's body sprawled across the bed, plunged them both into deep gloom.

"We're half asleep." Alistair yawned. "I suggest we try for the other half. There's nothing else we can do tonight."

CHAPTER 17

"IT'S LIKE THIS," IMELDA SAID, POURING COFFEE. "I have to fly around so much on my assignments that I'm kind of friendly with most of the pilots and crews on the flights——" She broke off to frown abstractedly at Marvin, the tip of her nose twitching.

"Oh dear," Stacey apologized. "The children didn't get their baths last night and I'm afraid we dashed off so fast this morning to get here that I just didn't think of it again."

"No, no," Imelda said. "It's only that I was wondering if you'd like some pastries with your coffee. I see he's brought his snack, but I think Danish are so much nicer than cheese crackers, don't you?"

"Great," Marvin said. He patted the package bulging out his pocket. "That's for later, anyhow."

Imelda darted into the kitchen, returning with a plate of Danish pastries, to which had been added a few sugar doughnuts. Alistair brightened perceptibly. Breakfast had been hurried and rather unsatisfactory since they hadn't wanted to linger for more than the basic minimum.

Marvin, as though mindful of that fact and not knowing when the next burst of speed would be required, took a pastry in one hand, a doughnut in the other, and alternated bites ignoring Stacey's reproving frown. His hands, she noticed with resigned despair, were distinctly grubby. He appeared to have taken the moratorium on bathing as a total dispensation from any association with soap and water. She was relieved to note that Hortense was still presentable.

"Everyone okay now?" Imelda asked.

"Fine, thank you." Alistair paused delicately. "You *did* have something to tell us?"

"It's like this," Imelda resumed. "I got to thinking that maybe Roger—he was the pilot on that flight—might have noticed something. So I telephoned and, luckily, I caught him on a stopover and we went out to dinner.

"Oh, I didn't tell him anything about your trouble," she added hastily. "I thought probably the less he knew about it, the better—for him. The crew has already been put through the wringer because that stewardess got herself killed. In fact, once we started talking about that, I didn't have to ask him any questions at all. It came pouring out and it's a wonder someone didn't murder her a long time ago. If ever a girl was asking for trouble, she was. And, in my line of work, you get to be an expert on these girls asking for trouble."

"It was apparent that she wasn't keeping the best of company," Alistair murmured. "Once she was away from the airline, that is."

"She certainly wasn't! But you don't know the half of it. Neither do the police, but they're trying to find out. Roger says they kept on about it so much that he regretted he'd told them anything at all. But the whole cockpit crew knew because they were all there when she came in to get him to radio ahead to Heathrow. So one of them was bound to have mentioned it, if he didn't. It isn't every day they carry a policeman and criminal aboard.''

"I told you so," Marvin said. "I told you those guys with the handcuffs did it!"

"Only they were both criminals, as it turned out," Imelda said. "The police had no extradited criminal coming in. They hadn't had an extradition case for months."

"It's the perfect cover," Alistair said. "They get special treatment at the airport. No passports, waved through Immigration, and then who checks on whether or not the waiting car actually delivers them to a police station or to a hideout in this country?"

"All it takes," Imelda said, "is one accomplice on the flight who can get the pilot to radio ahead to say they're carrying this extradition case and—"

"Lola Smith!" Stacey said.

"That's it. Roger and the others trusted her. So when she came into the cockpit and said she'd seen the extradition papers, why should they think she was lying? They took her word for it and radioed ahead."

"Then all the two men had to do was walk off and disappear." Alistair shook his head, half admiring the brazenness of it. "Those handcuffs were a nice touch. They'd have removed any lingering doubt and also guaranteed that they got seats by themselves. The other passengers would be too nervous or too embarrassed to sit near them.''

"I wouldn't be, Al,'' Marvin said.

"You're not the typical airlines passenger, Marvin. There aren't many like you.''

Marvin gave him a suspicious glance, sensing mockery, but Alistair was more concerned to follow through on his original train of thought.

"I wonder if Lola Smith made a habit—or a business—or helping criminals in and out of the country. If so, no wonder she was murdered. Especially if she decided to add blackmail to her lucrative little sidelines.''

"Then the jewellery might have had nothing to do with it at all,'' Stacey said thankfully. The fear that her carelessness might have contributed to Lola Smith's death had been hanging over her.

"And I am not to blame!'' Hortense exclaimed with equal gratitude, betraying a secret guilt.

"'Course you're not,'' Marvin said quickly. "It's not your fault if a bunch of crooks start killing each other.''

Alistair had been about to add something else but, at the sight of Hortense's radiant, relieved face, he closed his mouth again. Over the heads of the children, he met Stacey's eyes and she knew that her optimism was unfounded.

Criminals were notoriously opportunistic. When the two men had realized that a fortune in jewels was within grasping distance, it would have taken them very little time to formulate a plan. The fact that Lola Smith possessed a similar hat-box and was already their accomplice simply made things easier for them.

"They must have thought it was Christmas," Alistair risked muttering, as Hortense and Marvin wandered over to the window.

"And I was Santa Claus!" Stacey said bitterly. She should have been more on her guard, once the contents of the hat-box had been revealed. Especially with at least one known criminal on board. But the fact that he had been handcuffed to another man who was presumably a policeman had lulled her into a false sense of security. He had not seemed a threat because he was already in custody. How could anyone have guessed that both men were criminals?

"Were they confidence men, do you know?" Alistair asked Imelda. "Or was there a history of violence?"

"No one knows! They don't even know who the men were yet. The stewardess who could identify them is dead. They're waiting for a couple of other stewardesses on the flight to be routed back through Heathrow again so that they can try for a description."

"I could describe those guys, Al." Marvin turned away from the window. "I'll bet I could make a Photofit picture of both of them. Except—" his enthusiasm waned— "we don't want to go near the police, do we?"

"We'd rather not," Alistair agreed.

"Speaking of which, I ought to telephone Cousin Eustace," Stacey said. "Just so that he doesn't think we've run off permanently with his car. I can tell him we've got Hortense back and—" Her voice trailed off; she found that she had come to the end of her inspiration. How could she tell him that they suspected him of being in league with Hortense's would-be kidnapper and they intended to retain his car for as long as it suited them?

"I agree some sort of interim message to keep Cousin Eustace from going to the police might be a good idea," Alistair said. "Tell him Hortense is safe with us, but that we can't return immediately to resume enjoyment of his hospitality because . . ." He faltered for a moment, then continued triumphantly, "Because I have to stay in Town to attend an important audition—he'll believe anything of me. Apologize, but say this job is frightfully important to my career and we'll get his car back to him as soon as possible. Perhaps," he added thoughtfully, "we ought to pause somewhere along the way and send flowers to our hostess in the meantime."

"It will take more than flowers to square us with Eustace and Rowena," Stacey forecast gloomily.

"You can use my telephone," Imelda offered.

"I must say I'm disappointed in you, Cousin Eustacia," Eustace said icily. "Gravely disappointed."

"I'm sorry, Cousin Eustace. But it's awfully important that Alistair goes to this audition—his whole future could be at stake." She pulled the telephone closer, as though proximity could convey earnestness. The movement dislodged something small, which skittered towards her. She caught it before it fell to the floor.

"Yes, yes—" Eustace brushed aside something so unimportant as Alistair's future. "But I must remind you that we look to you to honor your commitments."

"I promise you, we'll bring your car back as soon as

possible and then—'' she nearly choked on the social lie—''we'll have a lovely visit with you.''

''I trust so. I may say that I thought, when you didn't return—and with your cases still in your rooms—''

''I can see that it must have been a worry for you. I'm terribly sorry. It—it took us quite a time to retrieve Hortense—'' (Did he know differently?) ''And then, we just weren't anywhere near a telephone. And when we did find one, Alistair had to call his agent before we did anything else—'' (Was she embroidering too much?) ''And he had news of this wonderful job, so we had to come straight back to London and—''

''Quite,'' Eustace said, in a tone of utter disbelief. ''You must proceed at your own pace, of course. Don't worry about us, we're quite content to await your convenience.''

''I knew you'd understand.'' Stacey ignored the heavy irony. ''And thank you so much for the use of your car. I'll try to repay you some day—''

Still talking, she replaced the receiver, but not before she had heard Eustace's rejoinder. She could not have heard it correctly.

Incredibly, it had sounded like, ''See that you do.''

''Well . . .'' Stacey turned from the phone to the row of waiting faces. ''I won't say he's exactly gruntled, but I think I've put off the evil moment of paying the piper for a little while longer.'' (''*See that you do.*'' Could he really have said that? What threat lay behind the words?)

''Every little bit helps,'' Alistair said. ''At least, I won't have to keep an eye on the driving mirror to see if the police are on our tail.''

"There's that, of course." There was something else, too. She became aware that she was still absently playing with the object that had been lodged under Imelda's telephone and that there was something strange about it. Small as it was, it was jointed and moved in an up and down motion in response to her fingertips. She glanced down curiously and froze with horror and disbelief.

It was the gold Nodding Donkey from Barbara Donaldson's charm bracelet.

Imelda hadn't noticed. She was standing there, smiling pleasantly at them, obviously waiting for them to leave. "I'm awfully glad I was able to help you," she said. "You must let me know how you make out."

So helpful, Imelda. But how did they know they could trust her?

Stacey's hand closed over the trinket as she tried to remember whether it had been on Barbara's charm bracelet the last time they had seen her. It was impossible, of course. They had had far too much on their minds to be concerned with a charm bracelet. And yet, each charm had a special meaning for Barbara, surely she would have mentioned it if she had lost one of them.

Unless, of course, she had not noticed that she had lost it until after they had parted. Just after they discovered Lola Smith's body. Could it have slipped off Barbara's bracelet while they were searching Lola's flat?

But how had it turned up in Imelda's flat?

There was a possible answer; one that Stacey did not want to contemplate. Imelda had been in Lola's flat after they had left it and picked up the charm there.

But that would mean that Imelda was in league with

the killers. And yet she seemed so kind and helpful; she also had an excellent career of her own and earned a great deal of money.

Of course, there were people who never felt that they had enough money. And Imelda was in a profession with a self-limiting span of success. A few years at the top and then new faces were wanted, sometimes even before the old faces had time to show the marks of age. Imelda might be minded to salt away as much money as possible against that evil day—no matter how she got it.

"What's the matter?" Alistair asked. "You're looking rather odd."

They were all staring at her. Perhaps it was better to face Imelda with it right now. Stacey opened her hand and held it out to them, the Nodding Donkey glittering in the center of her palm.

"That's Aunt Barbie's!" Hortense's face lit up. "That's her Nodding Donkey. But—" she raised her head and looked around—"where is she?"

"So it is!" Imelda pounced on it. "We looked everywhere. Where did you find it?"

"Under the telephone," Stacey said faintly. "I didn't know you knew Barbara Donaldson."

"So that's where it went. She came to tea yesterday and—" A strange look crossed Imelda's face. "What's the matter?"

"Barbara Donaldson flew to Abu Dhabi to meet her husband the day after we landed."

"She couldn't have. She was here." Imelda looked at Stacey incredulously. "You don't believe me, do you?"

"I don't know," Stacey said.

"I saw Aunt Barbie at the Marina after you said she had gone," Hortense reminded them. "I *know* I did!"

"That's right," Imelda said. "That was where I ran into her. She was sort of at a loose end and had several days to kill in London, so I invited her round."

"Then why didn't you mention it?"

"She made me promise not to. We discussed you a bit, I'm afraid. That plane journey was really all we had in common and—" Imelda broke off. "No matter what I say, you're not going to believe me, are you?"

"It does seem as though *someone* has been lying," Alistair said. "Why should Barbara Donaldson have told us she was leaving the country when she wasn't?"

"I think," Imelda said slowly, "she didn't want to get any more involved. Lots of people wouldn't."

"She *did* say her husband would be upset if he knew," Stacey admitted.

"There you are!" Imelda said. "And there was something else about her husband, too. She told me he was in Aberdeen and you say she told you that he was in Abu Dhabi."

"Perhaps he commuted," Alistair suggested.

"Perhaps, but I've run into a lot of these oil people," Imelda said. "They're secretive. Especially if they think there's a big strike in the offing. They'll do anything to keep word of it secret. He's probably somewhere in this country and Barbara was terrified of being caught up in any publicity and giving him away."

It was possible. Stacey saw her own doubt mirrored in Alistair's face. They absorbed the idea in silence. No one could blame Barbara for wanting to escape further involvement—particularly after the discovery of Lola Smith's body. And if the multinational oil interests of her husband were at stake as well...

Losing interest, Marvin had wandered back to the window with Hortense. They stood whispering behind the curtain, looking down on the street, obviously wishing themselves down there and away from this flat. It was a feeling Stacey sympathized with.

"We'd like to thank _you_ for all your trouble," Alistair said. "You've been very kind... and patient."

"We going now, Al?" Marvin caught the note in his voice and hurried back from the window, Hortense trailing after him.

"I think it's time we did," Alistair said.

High time. They had learned what they had come here for—and more. But they could not discuss it here.

"Thank you again," Stacey said in her best social manner. "You've been a great help."

"Think nothing of it." Imelda ushered them to the door. "I only wish I could have done more."

After several more protestations of gratitude and disclaimers, the door finally closed behind them. Even the children breathed sighs of relief.

"That went a bit sticky toward the last," Alistair led the way to the lift. "What do you think?"

"Hey, Al—" Marvin was hanging back, now he stopped abruptly. "Al, is there a back door out of this joint?"

"There must be." Alistair looked at him with sudden sharp unease. "Why?"

"Because I think we ought to use it. Those handcuff guys are waiting for us out front."

CHAPTER 18

THE BASEMENT WAS DIVIDED INTO A SMALL LAUNDRY room and a large underground garage with numbered parking bays for the residents.

"Pity we didn't know about this on the way in." Alistair's voice echoed back at him and he winced. "We might have been able to leave the car here," he ended on a lower note. "Now it looks as though we'll have to abandon it."

"But what about Cousin Eustace?"

"*Eustace . . . stace . . .*" the walls threw back.

"We can't argue here," Alistair said. "We'll send Eustace a postcard and let him collect the car."

"Let's go in here a minute—" Marvin opened the door of the deserted laundry room. "There's something I want to tell you."

"I don't think I can bear to hear any more," Alistair muttered, but they followed Marvin into the room. It was a considerably better place than the garage for a discussion. There was no echo and also, Stacey realized, no place where anyone could be concealed to eavesdrop on them.

"Right!" Alistair surveyed the room, then turned to Marvin. "What is it now?"

"Listen, Al," Marvin said. "I've had a great idea."

"Is that all you want to tell us?"

"It's a really great idea."

"Then it can wait." Alistair started for the door. "I thought you meant you had some solid information. Perhaps you'd spotted someone waiting outside the back door—"

"No, there's nobody out there, Al."

"Then let's get going before there is." Alistair caught Marvin's arm and tried to drag him along, but Marvin dug in his heels. "If Imelda is in this with them, she's had time to signal to them that we've left. When we don't come out the front entrance in a reasonable length of time, they're going to start investigating."

"Just let me tell you my idea, Al. It will work. It's really great!"

"Listen, Marvin." Alistair spoke with dangerous patience. "From what I have been able to gather of your checkered career, every time you have had a really great idea, it has ended in your being expelled from yet another military academy. I appreciate the fact that you have probably now run out of academies, but I think you're a little young to start being expelled from countries. Your father wouldn't like it. And, since your family solicitor placed me in nominal charge of you, I would have to answer to General Birnbaum for your conduct. And *I* wouldn't like *that*."

"I think it is a good idea," Hortense said.

"You keep out of this!" Alistair gave Marvin's arm a

tug that threatened to dislocate his shoulder. Marvin lost his balance and lurched forward. Stacey opened the door and the forward momentum carried them both through it. She caught up Hortense's hand and followed them.

"No noise!" Alistair warned as Marvin opened his mouth to protest. "Keep together. Move fast. And—" He gave Marvin a shake. "And no more trouble from you, young man."

"Okay, Al," Marvin said with suspicious docility. "Have it your way."

They tiptoed to the back door. Alistair checked outside quickly and beckoned them along. As they left the building, a car swung into the ramp leading down to the garage, further blocking them from view.

They crossed the street in a rush and turned down the first side street, then another, and another, losing themselves in the maze of narrow streets. With luck, losing any pursuers as well. When they looked back, they could still see Imelda's block of flats looming in the distance.

"Al—" Marvin said tentatively. "Al—I'm sorry, Al, but I've got to go to the john."

"Why," Alistair asked between clenched teeth, "didn't you mention that before we left Imelda's flat?"

"I didn't like to," Marvin said. "I mean, I didn't think we were getting along so good toward the end. It might have annoyed her."

"And you'd prefer to annoy me?" Alistair halted and tried to take his bearings. "I'm tempted to shove you behind the nearest tree and let you take your chances."

"Aw, Al, I'm too old for that. There's gotta be a john around here somewhere."

"I want to, too," Hortense chimed in. Her eyebrows lifted disdainfully. "And I will not use a tree."

"All right, all right," Alistair said. "Let me think."

Stacey looked over her shoulder. They still appeared too be perilously close to Imelda's flat. Were their stalkers still waiting for them to emerge from the entrance, or had they realized by now what had happened? Had the pursuit already started?

"A restaurant?" she suggested. "A department store?" Both appeared to be in short supply in this area.

"A pub," Alistair corrected. "That's all we're likely to find around here." He drew in a deep breath and blew it out with exasperation. "A personal appeal to the landlord sometimes works. You'll have to do it. You have the right accent—and you're prettier." He glanced at his watch. "They're open now. We'll try the first one we see."

The Bird-in-Hand was on the next corner. The landlord was sympathetic, but wary.

"If anyone says anything," he warned, "say that they're my niece and nephew. Rest-rooms are back there—" he gestured. "But please, be as quick as you can."

In gratitude, Alistair ordered a double Scotch and propped up the bar while Marvin went off on his own and Stacey decided it might not be a bad idea to accompany Hortense and take advantage of the facilities herself.

"What would you like?" Alistair greeted her on their returned.

"Nothing, thanks. Hortense can't stay in here and I'm not letting her wait outside on her own."

"Be with you as soon as Marvin comes back. Shouldn't

be long.'' Alistair tossed Hortense a packet of crisps and waved them on their way.

Stacey found herself pacing up and down beside the Saloon Bar door, ready to snatch up Hortense and carry her back inside if there should be any sign of their pursuers. Hortense, however, seemed completely at ease and untroubled by any worries, munching away happily at her crisps.

"Stacey?" Companionably she offered the bag of crisps, but Stacey shook her head.

"No, thanks, I'm not hungry."

"Oh?" Hortense looked slightly amazed at the quaint idea that one had to be hungry to want to eat crisps. With a shrug, she delved back into the bag herself. Clearly, hunger had nothing to do with it.

She would have time to grow hungry, Stacey reflected, if Marvin took much longer. Restlessly she moved to push open the frosted glass door to see if there were any signs of activity inside. She was nearly bowled over as Alistair shot through the door and glared at her accusingly.

"Where is he?" he demanded. "He isn't in the Gents, isn't he out here with you?"

"I haven't seen him." Stacey deduced that they could only be discussing Marvin. "I thought he was with you."

Hortense continued to plough her way through the crisps with a complacency that bordered on the nerve-racking. Particularly as there was no doubt that she had heard their conversation and knew exactly what was at stake.

"Hortense," Alistair said in sugared tones. "Hortense, do *you* know where Marvin is?"

"*Mais oui.*" Hortense tilted the bag to let the accumulation of crumbs and salt run into her palm. "Marvin has gone to solve the case." She raised her hand, parted her lips, and let the last savory fragments pour into her mouth.

"Oh, he has, has he?" Alistair fought for control. "And just how does he propose to achieve that?"

"*Très simple.*" Hortense swallowed and smiled up at him. "He will allow himself to be captured. Then he will discover exactly the position they occupy and what they wish to gain from us."

"He's done *what*?" Alistair's voice rose to a strangled shout.

"Marvin is very clever," Hortense said. "He will discover everything."

"If he survives long enough," Alistair said. He leaned against the wall of the pub and found Stacey already there. "He's out of his mind and this time he's gone too far."

"Marvin is very clever," Hortense reiterated. "He knows everything. I am going to marry him when we grow up." She paused. "He does not know that, of course."

"You're a very brave little girl," Alistair told her. "Not to say foolhardly. But, if we don't stop him, Marvin won't live to grow up."

"Marvin knows what he is doing . . . ?" Hortense's voice wavered. Without the presence of her idol, she appeared to have become aware that there might possibly be reason for doubt.

"Come on!" Alistair plunged between them, catching

up Hortense and Stacey by the hand and hurrying them
down the street. "If we hurry, we might catch him." He
propelled them at breakneck pace back along the way
they had come.

"He has gone," Hortense said with finality. "He said
that you are to go back to the flat in Sloane Square and
wait for his captors to contact you there."

"Shouldn't we take a taxi straight back to Sloane
Square?" Stacey gasped. "They might be trying to reach
us now."

"Then they're out of luck, aren't they?" Alistair
divided a bitter glance between her and Hortense. "If we
can't catch up with Marvin, at least we can repossess
Cousin Eustace's car. They'll be gone by now, if they've
got Marvin, and it will get us back there quicker than
public transport can."

He was right. Stacey lengthened her stride, aware that
poor Hortense was running to keep up with them, but
uncomplaining.

They were back at the block of flats so swiftly that she
wondered why they had taken so many turnings in their
effort to escape. It seemed that keeping to one straight
line had led them right back into the thick of things.

Except that the thick of things had moved. There was
no sign of anyone lurking in the vicinity. Nor of Marvin.

Cousin Eustace's car was still where they had left it
and, after circling it cautiously, Alistair gingerly swung
open the door by the driver's seat. Motioning them to
stay back, he got in, turned the ignition key and started
the engine. When nothing dire happened, he beckoned
them forward and into the car.

Stacey glanced upwards at Imelda's windows: no sign of life or interest there. Perhaps Imelda was innocent. Or perhaps she had left the flat and was even now with the kidnappers.

Further consideration was suspended as Alistair swung the car into the street at a dangerous speed and headed back towards Sloane Square.

It was almost an anti-climax to find the flat as they had left it. Years seemed to have passed. It would not have been a surprise to see cobwebs hanging from the ceiling and a thick mat of dust covering everything.

Instead, pale sunlight streamed in through clean glass windows, lighting up the signs of their recent departure. Stacey picked up an abandoned magazine, then stood holding it helplessly before letting it drop into a chair again. Alistair began pacing the floor, keeping close to the telephone.

Only Hortense seemed unconcerned. She headed for the kitchen with a purposeful air. There followed very shortly the sound of dishes rattling and the clatter of pans.

"She's happy, at any rate," Alistair said absently. "It must be nice to have such faith in someone else. Mind you, I think she's misplaced it. Marvin has bitten off more than he can chew this time."

"We really *will* have to call in the police," Stacey said. "We can't keep them out of it any longer."

"Rather what I was thinking myself. I'm afraid they're going to take a dim view of being kept out of it this long. Do you think," he added hopefully, "we ought to try to sort our story for them? I mean, smooth over some of the more awkward points?''

''How?''

The question opened a vast vista of unexplained and, by this time, unexplainable decisions. *Why* didn't you go to the police immediately the jewels disappeared? *Oh yes. You thought there had been a simple error and you could retrieve them without publicity?*

Then *why* hadn't you notified the police openly when you discovered Lola Smith's body? *Dear, dear, we are publicity-shy, aren't we, madam? Perhaps a bit oversensitive? After all, a First Family of Thringsby, Massachusetts, isn't exactly headline or Stop Press material over here. Now is it, madam?*

''Yes, I see what you mean.'' Alistair ran a hand over his rumpled brow. ''But we *must* be able to think of *something* to tell them.''

Something better than the truth, he meant.

''We could always try, '*Everything went black,*' '' she said, trying to control a laugh that threatened to become hysterical.

''That's all very well, as far as it goes,'' he said, with a seriousness that, in itself, verged on the hysterical. ''But then we have to account for the length of time the blackness persisted. I don't think we could justify it, short of pleading total amnesia—and there are too many of us for that. I've never heard that amnesia was contagious. We'll have to think of something else.''

There was silence while they both tried to think of something else.

"Come quickly!" Hortense appeared in the doorway. "There are letters coming through the mailbox."

"It must be the afternoon post," Alistair said. They followed him in some trepidation as he collected the three letters that lay on the mat beneath the mail slot.

"Silly, really," he commented, sorting through them automatically. "The days are long gone when anyone could post a letter in the morning and have it delivered that afternoon. There couldn't possibly be anything for us."

"Of course not," Stacey agreed. They drifted back toward the telephone.

"Oh—oh!" Alistair flourished the final letter. "Here's one for Marvin from Germany—and the handwriting looks as though it had been addressed by someone in a raging fury. Someone must have broken the news to the General. About Marvin's having been expelled from another military academy, I mean."

There was a gloomy silence as they contemplated what the next news to be broken to General Birnbaum about his own son might have to be.

Across the room, the telephone rang abruptly.

CHAPTER 19

"I TOLD YOU THIS WOULD WORK, AL." MARVIN'S voice was loud enough for all of them to hear.

"And I told you I wouldn't like it," Alistair replied. "Marvin, where are you?"

"Well . . . uh . . . I'm not sure. They've got me. They're standing right here next to me while I'm talking to you."

"That's why it was a rotten idea, Marvin. They've got you—and they'll want the jewels to ransom you. And we don't have the jewels. Now what do we do?"

"No, they don't, Al. Want the jewels, I mean. They've already got them."

"What?" Stacey shrieked. She grabbed for the phone. There was a brief, undignified tug-of-war which Alistair won by clasping her firmly to his side.

"Someone had to have them," Marvin pointed out reasonably. "And we'd checked everywhere else."

"What *do* they want then, Marvin?" Alistair asked patiently. "I assume they want something. They've been following us all along. They tried to kidnap Hortense. They've got you. They must want something out of us."

Perhaps they just want to dispose of all the witnesses.

Stacey met Alistair's eyes and saw that he had had the same thought. *Get us all together and arrange a fatal accident.*

"Yeah, I've been explaining to them," Marvin said carefully. "I told them Stacey is going back to the States and Hortense is going to France. I said you were going to Hollywood to make a film—"

So Marvin's mind had also been running along the same lines. Perhaps with more cause. How much had he been able to learn about his captors? So much that they could no longer afford to release him, if that had ever been their intention?

"And I told them nobody ever pays any attention to anything I say," Marvin finished, sounding dispirited.

"You've had a letter from your father." Alistair tried to cheer him. "Shall I open it and read it to you?"

"Naw. Just shake it and see if any money falls out." For a moment, Marvin sounded like his old self. "I gotta go now, Al. They want to talk to you."

"And I want to talk to them," Alistair said grimly. "Chin up, Marvin. It will be all right."

"Sure, Al," Marvin said. "Don't worry. I've got plenty of sugar left."

"Nothing you could have said would have worried me more. For God's sake, Marvin, keep away from their petrol tank. You're in no position to antagonize them!" But Alistair was speaking to a silent line.

"You've heard the boy." Another voice came on the line. "He's safe and well. There's no reason he can't stay that way—if you'll only cooperate."

"What do you want?" Alistair asked.

"You have a car, I understand." He didn't wait for an answer. "There's a road cutting through Regent's Park from the Outer Circle, Chester Road to the Inner Circle around Queen Mary's Gardens. You know it?" This time, he paused for a reply.

"I know it."

"Then go there. Just keep driving slowly around the Inner Circle until we flag you down. And don't do anything silly, like bringing the police into this."

"We haven't so far," Alistair reminded him.

"So you haven't." There was a brief indefinable sound that might have been a chuckle. "That's why we may be able to do business. Oh, and one other thing—" The sudden elaborate casualness betrayed that this was the point of the whole exercise.

"Yes?"

"Have the woman bring along the stuff she took from Lola's flat. Everything—case and all."

"How many miniatures of brandy were there, do you remember?" Stacey was frantically working to reconstruct the contents of the hat-box. "We've drunk some. And cigarettes—we've been smoking them." She shook her head in despair. "We'll never be able to get it all back together again."

"It just has to pass a quick muster," Alistair encouraged. He had retrieved several of the miniature bottles from the waste bin, filled them with water and planted them in the bottom cartons. There was not a great deal they could do about the missing cigarettes.

"I doubt if they give a damn about this stuff," he said.

"I think it's meant as a smokescreen. Let's just hope that it's a good sign that they're bothering about smoke-screens. It may signify that they're going to let us go our own ways after they've collected the stuff."

"With the jewels," Stacey said bitterly. "They've still got the Orpington Bequest and I shouldn't think they're going to swap it for this."

"No, I'm afraid not," Alistair agreed. "I can't see them parting with anything of value. I'm not sure what we can do about that. Nothing, until we've got Marvin back, at any rate. Then, perhaps, the police—"

"We should have gone to them in the first place."

"Too late to worry about that now." Alistair stepped back and surveyed the hat-box. "That looks about right. Just two more items—but I suspect those may be what they're really after."

"What?"

"The diary and the list she had buried underneath all this. You still have them, haven't you?" He held out his hands. "Hortense, find me some paper, please."

"Here." Stacey pulled the diary and sheets of paper from the bottom of her handbag and tried to smooth the papers. They had not been so rumpled when she had removed them from the hat-box. "What are you going to do?"

"I'm going to copy the diary entries and the list before we turn everything over to them. That way, we'll have something, at least, to show the police. Perhaps they'll be able to make more of it than we can."

"Suppose there are microdots on the original—" Stacey

ran her fingertips over the list, but, apart from the wrinkles, it seemed quite smooth.

"I doubt if they went in for anything so elaborate," Alistair reassured her. "I think the message is the message and not the medium. Presumably it has some meaning for them."

He accepted paper and pen from Hortense with a nod of thanks and began copying swiftly. "We can make a couple more copies later and study them. But it seemed a perfectly straightforward list of passenger names and addresses and a few diary notes too cryptic to be code. Just Lola's personal shorthand, I'd say." He frowned and looked up.

"I'm not too happy about your coming along," he admitted. "I think you ought to stay here."

"They're expecting to see me," Stacey said. "But I think we ought to leave Hortense behind."

"*Non!*" Hortense pouted. "I go with you. I do not stay alone here. They will expect me, too. They know we are all together."

"You may be right," Alistair admitted. "If one of us is missing, they may suspect a trick and not make contact. Then we'd have the waiting to do all over again until they decided to have another try."

And meanwhile they'd have Marvin. Stacey shuddered involuntarily.

"Hurry," she said.

They had circled around the Garden for the fourth time when Hortense announced quietly from the back seat, "I think we are being followed."

"Bloody well about time," Alistair grumbled. "I thought we were going to be kept circling all night."

"They haven't signalled yet," Stacey said. "It might not be them. It's a public thoroughfare, any number of innocent cars may be using the road."

"I can see Marvin!" Hortense bounced up and down excitedly. "He is there in the car!"

"And they're gaining on us." Alistair slowed hopefully. "It's their play now."

The car swept past. Marvin and Hortense waving wildly to each other. Once in front of them, it slowed, then accelerated again.

"I think we're meant to follow them," Alistair said. He blinked his lights in compliance.

They circled the Garden once more, then the car ahead drew in at the most deserted spot on the road. Alistair pulled in behind cautiously, leaving a good distance between them.

"We might want to get out of here in a hurry," he said, "and we don't want them blocking our way. Hortense, you stay in the car." He glanced at Stacey as though he would like to give her the same order, but she shook her head and opened the door on her side. He shrugged and got out, coming round swiftly to her side. They moved a short distance toward the other car and then stood waiting.

It seemed an interminable time before one of the doors opened in the car ahead of them and a heavy dark figure stepped out and advanced toward them. Another figure remained in the car, dropped over the steering-wheel. Marvin stayed motionless in the back seat, although the white blur of his face turned toward them. They could not see his expression.

The man was vaguely familiar. Armed with foreknowledge, she recognized him as one of the men who had been handcuffed together on board the jet. His air of command—now looking more like arrogance—marked him as the one they had assumed to be the policeman in charge of the supposed prisoner.

"Let's have it." The man held out his hand for the hat-box Stacey was carrying.

"Let's have Marvin first," Alistair said.

"You're in no position to dictate terms. You get him after we make sure we've got what we want."

Stacey broke the deadlock by thrusting the hat-box at him. For an instant she considered apologizing because they had used some of the contents, then stopped herself. Better to be silent and not give them the idea that the contents had been examined in any way.

"Now you're being sensible." He took the hat-box and retreated several paces. "My partner has a gun," he warned them, as he took his eyes off them to open the hat-box and inspect it.

"I'm not a hero unless I have a stunt man to double for me," Alistair said.

"Keep it that way." What he saw in the hat-box appeared to satisfy the man as much as Alistair's attitude. He gave a nod and backed toward the waiting car.

"Marvin," Alistair reminded him. "We delivered the goods, now we want Marvin back."

"In good time. Suppose you go back to the flat and

wait for him. We'll let him go soon and he can find his own way home.''

"His father is an American General,'' Alistair warned. "If any harm comes to Marvin, it will have international repercussions. And Interpol will make the world too hot to hold you.''

"So he's told us.''

There was a flurry of activity in the other car. Stacey caught her breath. The man, who had been intent on watching Alistair, sensed that something was happening. He whirled and began running toward the car.

Just as he reached it, the car quivered and exploded with a dull metallic "Crump!''

"Oh my God!'' Alistair said, not seeming to notice that he had been knocked to his knees. "Marvin!''

"Marvin!'' Stacey echoed, tears starting. She, too, was on her hand and knees.

Ahead of them, the man who had been running toward the car lay on the road, ominously still. The hat-box, unharmed, rolled like a hoop across the road and settled on the far side.

"Marvin!'' Alistair struggled to his feet and helped Stacey up. "How am I ever going to explain this to General Birnbaum?''

"He was such a sweet boy,'' Stacey sobbed. "Really he was.''

"Poor Marvin,'' Alistair agreed. "He wasn't bad. Just impetuous. He had a brilliant career ahead of him—I'm not sure at what, but brilliant.''

Behind them, Stacey heard the car door slam. "Hortense!'' she said. "This will be a terrible shock for her.''

"I'm not exactly accustomed to this sort of thing myself," Alistair said.

"Hey, you guys!" A familiar voice spoke at Stacey's elbow. "We'd better get out of here before the cops come along."

"Marvin?" She flung her arms around him in relief.

"I told you everything would be okay." He squirmed away. "Here, I got this for you."

"Marvin!" She accepted the hat-box; the weight told her that this was the right one. "The Oprington Bequest!"

"Sure," he said. "I couldn't leave it with them, could I?"

"Oh, Marvin?" Ridiculously, she was crying harder than ever.

"I was not worried," Hortense said complacently, firmly attached to Marvin's side. "I knew Marvin would be all right."

"Which is more than can be said for the other people." Alistair herded them back into their own car. "I assume you had something to do with that explosion, Marvin? It has all the hallmarks of your work."

"It was easy, Al," Marvin said. "All you need for explosives is some chemical fertilizer and a couple of other simple ingredients. I told you I'm going to be a scientist—"

"Fertilizer—' Stacey gave a final dab to her eyes, feeling a lot better. "There was a truckload of chemical fertilizer at that pub—and you got hold of the box of cheese crackers—"

"It was empty, honest it was," Marvin said. "She was only going to throw it away. So I took it and filled it with the fertilizer. I figured it would probably come in handy, the way things were going."

"Marvin," Alistair said thoughtfully. "Promise me you'll never become a defector and go over to the other side. We need you here."

"Well, sure, Al," Marvin said. "You oughta know better than to say such a thing."

"Hmmm." Alistair started the motor and swung into a U-turn so that they needn't drive past the shattered car. "Tell me, Marvin, do you usually carry around the components for explosives, just in case?"

"Well, the main one—apart from the chemical fertilizer— is sugar. I always have lots of sugar on me. I told you, it's sort of my hobby. You can do an awful lot with sugar."

"*You* can, Marvin." Alistair drove out of the park. "I know there's a health faction that claims refined sugar is one of the most dangerous substances known to man, but you've added a whole new dimension to that theory."

CHAPTER 20

STACEY INSISTED ON DELIVERING THE ORPINGTON BEquest to the museum officials immediately. There, pleading excessive jet lag to excuse the delay, she had handed it over with a minimum of polite conversation and escaped back to the others in the waiting car.

"My father—" Marvin had been studying his letter in her absence—"wants me to try Sandhurst. I don't want to go to Sandhurst, Al."

"I'm sure it's mutual, Marvin. Porton Down is more your style."

"Yeah." Marvin brightened. "He's coming back next week. Why don't you talk to him and tell him that, Al?"

"That's over!" Stacey broke up the discussion, slamming the car door behind her, feeling curiously deflated. "Now I suppose we'd better return this car to Cousin Eustace." She swallowed and amended, "I mean, *I'll* do it. He's my cousin, after all."

"We might as well come along," Alistair said easily, heading the car towards Guildford. "It will only confuse Cousin Eustace if you suddenly appear in your own *persona* as a single woman. You'll have enough explaining to do, as it is."

"Marvin—" Stacey remembered something else that needed explaining. "Let me see that picture you thought was of me."

"Here you are." Marvin found it and handed it to her. "It *is* you, isn't it?"

"Yes." She was walking down the path, the Orpington Memorial Museum in the background. "But I've never seen it before. I don't know when it was taken, or how Cousin Eustace came into possession of it. Or why."

"Obviously," Alistair said, "he had it in order to identify you. He'd never seen you, either."

"How curious." Alistair's solution seemed the correct

one. "It would appear that Cousin Eustace has some explaining of his own to do."

"I found out some answers," Marvin said. Cousin Eustace was not of immediate importance to him. "Those guys were talking in front of me, kinda roundabout. They thought I wouldn't know what they were talking about. They must," he added in disgust, "have thought I was just a kid."

"No one who really knew you," Alistair reassured him solemnly, "would ever think that, Marvin."

"They were part of a gang." Marvin ignored the jibe with a long-suffering air. "And they had this racket going with Lola Smith. She gave them the names and addresses of first-class passengers and told them how long they were going to be out of the country on their holidays— she found out by chatting to the passengers. Then the gang burgled their houses while they were away. It was supposed to be a sort of percentage deal, but they never really gave Lola Smith all the money that was due her and, of course, she couldn't check up on them."

"I can quite see it might be a bit difficult to ring up former passengers who'd been burgled and ask them how much they'd lost," Alistair said. "It might start them thinking."

"That's right," Marvin said. "The way it was, they'd never get together and discover what they had in common was travelling on a jet where she was a stewardess. Everybody just thought they'd been unlucky and burglars had been watching the house, or maybe they'd forgotten to cancel the milk or newspapers, or something like that gave them away."

"Practically foolproof," Alistair agreed.

"Yeah, until they tried to cheat her over the jewels and tell her they weren't worth much. She'd actually *seen* those—"

Hortense gave a small guilty whimper.

"—and so she had a pretty good idea of what they were worth. They started fighting and she threatened to give them away to the police—"

"'When thieves fall out . . .'" Alistair said.

"Yeah." Marvin nodded gloomily. "So they killed her. Only, after they'd made their getaway with the jewels, they remembered that they had to get hold of her latest list because if the police found it they might start figuring things out. Only by that time we'd been there and taken the hat-box away. They saw us leaving with it and they followed us to try to get it back. Only we moved around a lot."

"You're learning understatement." Alistair swung the car into the final lap of the journey. "At least, the hat-box is with the wrecked car now. The police can start putting two and two together and question them when the doctor allows it."

"You don't think—" Stacey suggested hesitantly—"that perhaps we ought to make another anonymous telephone call to sort of push the police in the right direction?"

"No!"

"No!"

"No!" It was a unanimous veto.

"I think we'd better keep out of it," Alistair said. "We've been lucky, but one more phone call would be crowding our luck."

"Yeah," Marvin said. "The cops might start figuring ›ut too much. Let's quit while we're ahead."

"All right. It was only a suggestion." Stacey found hat she was relieved to have been over-ruled. The ‹mpending interview with Cousin Eustace threatened to ›e awkward enough without adding any further complica-:ions.

"I'm disappointed in you, Cousin Eustacia. Very disap-›ointed, indeed."

It was obvious that, once he had a grievance, Cousin Eustace did not dismiss it lightly. The fact that it was a justified grievance and she was utterly in the wrong did 1ot mitigate Stacey's growing resentment. There was no 1eed to speak to her as though she were an obstreperous :hild.

In fact, Eustace had not even addressed Marvin or Hortense in that manner. He had hardly noticed when Hortense had slipped past him and dashed upstairs to ‑etrieve her belongings. She was back now, triumphantly ‹lutching her own hat-box.

"Well, let it go, let it go." Belatedly, Cousin Eustace ›eemed to sense Stacey's mood and dredged up a placa-:ory smile. "We'll say no more about it. It's not for me ‹o say, in any case. I have a little surprise for you. And ›ou, I can see—" his smile broadened and became more ›enuine—"have a little surprise for me."

Before anyone could move, he reached out and took :he hat-box from Hortense and placed it on the table. His ›mile disappeared as he snapped open the lid and looked ‹nside.

"What's this?" he roared in outrage. "What are you playing at now?"

"This is Pierrot." Hortense came forward to reclaim and introduce her toys. "And this is Suzette—"

"Never mind that!" He pushed aside her hand and upended the hat box, spilling the toys across the table. "Where is the Orpington Treasure?"

"At the Duvanov Exhibition, of course." Stacey could not keep a hint of relieved triumph out of her voice. "Where it's supposed to be."

"The Exhibition!" Eustace's face turned puce. "What *is* this? What," he demanded again, "are you playing at?"

"See here," Alistair tried to intervene. "I don't think we know what *you're* playing at."

"I certainly don't," Stacey said. "Why shouldn't the Orpington Bequest be at the Exhibition? That was the whole point of my trip."

"Bequest!" Eustace doubled his fists and struck the table with them. "Thringsby!" he bellowed. "*Thringsby!*"

Stacey stared at him in blank amazement, thinking for a wild moment that he was calling down imprecations upon her birthplace.

The door behind Eustace Orpington-Blaine opened silently and Rowena advanced hesitatingly into the room. She was followed by Gordon Thringsby.

"Gordon!" Stacey could not believe it. "What are you doing here?"

"Never mind that!" Gordon gave her a most unfriendly look. "What are *you* doing is more to the point. What is this story you're telling about several husbands? Who

is this man?'' His unfriendly gaze encompassed Alistair.
"And where—'' it roamed on across the children—"where
did you collect these—these *guttersnipes*?''

Hortense and Marvin drew together in mutual outrage.
Hortense brushed defensively at a patch of dust on her
skirt and pulled a loose thread from a place where an
epaulette had once rested on Marvin's shoulder. Marvin
placed a sheltering arm around her and glared back at
Gordon.

"Who the hell are *you*?'' Marvin demanded. "And
where do you get off calling *us* names?''

"My question precisely,'' Alistair put in.

Suddenly they were all looking at Stacey. All except
Cousin Eustace who, still in a rage, had stooped and was
dragging a heavy chest out from beneath the table.

"This is Gordon Thringsby.'' Stacey felt there was a
certain weakness in her introduction. "He's Curator of
the Orpington Memorial Museum,'' she added. "In
Thringsby, Massachusetts.''

"One of *the* Thringsbys, no doubt,'' Alistair murmured.

"As a matter of fact, I am,'' Gordon said. "And just
who are you? And what are you doing here with my
fiancée?''

"Shall we just say I'm escorting her?''

"He's been helping me,'' Stacey corrected. "They all
have. Oh, Gordon, I've been having the most awful
time!''

"Never mind that now.'' Cousin Eustace straightened
and glared accusingly at Gordon. "I want to know what's
going on here. You gave me to understand that Cousin
Eustacia had every sympathy with my position and was

prepared to be cooperative. From the moment I met her, I began to suspect that nothing was farther from the truth. She didn't even seem to know what I was talking about.''

"I didn't get a chance to brief her thoroughly enough," Gordon said. "It will be all right."

"All right? Didn't you hear her? She's turned the Orpington Treasure over to the Exhibition. It will be on display when the Exhibition opens. What about that?"

"Yes, unfortunate," Gordon agreed. "However, I'm sure that—"

"And—" Eustace kicked open the lid of the chest— "what about *this*?"

Inside, the Orpington Bequest glittered as the light struck it. There was a swift intake of breath from Alistair and the children, but Stacey felt as though she might never breathe again.

"I thought she was playing the game," Eustace continued accusingly, "although rather strangely, when she dashed off with her friends, leaving her hat-box here. But when I opened it to make the switch, there was nothing in it. Nothing but a child's junk! No jewellery at all. It was sheer mockery—and insult."

"Jeez," Marvin said softly. "These guys are worse crooks than the ones that have been chasing us!"

Switch! The word penetrated Stacey's numbed mind and she looked more closely at the Orpington Bequest. On second, more thoughtful, inspection the jewels did not sparkle quite so brightly. Paste, rather than genuine gems. Not the Bequest, but a very clever copy. Probably made at the same time, as was common in those days, for occasions not grand enough to warrant the genuine regalia. A really close scrutiny would undoubtedly reveal the silver foil backing the smaller, more inferior paste stones, and the setting would be pinchbeck. But the copies would be good enough to fool anyone not familiar with the genuine Orpington Bequest—or casual visitors to the Museum who didn't know the difference, in any case.

"Unfortunate," Gordon said again, "but perhaps just as well. I always feared it might be dangerous to palm off copies on the Exhibition. They would not only recognize fakes immediately, but it might give rise to questions as to when the switch had been made—"

"I told you. Any questions and the Orpingtons would claim that the jewellery had never left the family. We could then prove it by producing the genuine articles and explaining that we had never bothered to prosecute Lady Orpington for the return of the gems because they *were* the fake set—"

"Which she, in the haste of her departure, had packed, not noticing that they were the wrong set?" Stacey's voice shook between indignation and laughter. "No one who had ever known Great-Grand-Aunt Eustacia would believe that for a minute."

"Ah, but no one we're dealing with has ever met her." Eustace looked at Stacey with dislike. "Nor had they ever seen the Orpington Treasures—either genuine or copy—that's the whole point."

"It will be far better this way," Gordon said. "We can make the exchange after the Exhibition closes. They'll have had the real thing on display, so they'll be happy. And who's to say when the exchange took place—if the substitution is ever noticed. Which, I may say, is highly unlikely. No one in Thringsby will ever know the difference.''

"I will," Stacey said softly, sadly.

"You?" Cousin Eustace gave her a look which said plainly that she did not count. "That won't matter. A wife can't testify against her husband."

"You're gonna marry that creep?" Marvin asked incredulously.

"I do not think you should," Hortense said. "I do not like him."

"Stacey, get *rid* of these brats!" Gordon hissed.

"I don't see why I should," Stacey said. "They're making more sense than you are. *And* Cousin Eustace," she added bitterly.

"Stacey—" Gordon smiled, abruptly becoming conciliatory. "I think we need to have a nice quiet *private* conversation. Why don't we go into another room and—"

"Because I don't want to," Stacey said. "I want to stay here with my friends."

"But, Stacey—" Gordon's smile became strained. "*I'm* your friend—"

"Are you?" The memory of their conversation the night before she flew to Heathrow returned to her. "You kept asking me if I minded about the museum getting the Orphington Bequest," she said. "I thought you were worried about my feelings, or perhaps wondering if I were honest enough to be trusted as courier. You were, all right, but you were trying to sound me out to discover whether I'd be willing to go along with you in your dirty little scheme to defraud the museum."

"Stacey!" Gordon drew himself up. "There's no need to speak to me like that!"

"There's every need! It's the truth!" Stacey took a deep breath and brought her voice back under control. She was conscious of Alistair's approving nod.

"I'm sorry you choose to take that attitude," Gordon said stiffly.

"You tried to make me an accessory to fraud and grand larceny! What attitude did you expect me to take?"

"I expected you to be reasonable. It's true—" he halfway apologized—"that we hadn't a chance to discuss this properly. But you know in your heart that the Orpington Bequest should have gone to you. It was only the overweening vanity of a cantankerous old woman that brought it to the museum—where it's totally wasted. No one in Thringsby appreciates it or cares about it. We can't afford to advertise it as an attraction to people who might care because that would draw unwelcome attention to it and we can't afford the premiums to insure it against theft.

"I'm taking what I see as a sensible course and I wish you could see it that way, too. Thringsby will be just as happy with the replica set—which is not without value in itself. It was created in the same workshop at the same time—a not uncommon procedure and is not without artistic and historic interest."

"Precisely," Cousin Eustace said with satisfaction. "We can make the exchange when the Exhibition closes and you'll fly back to the States with the replica set. No bones broken, the genuine set is back in the family— where it belongs—and, of course, there'll be a nice little sweetener for you and Mr. Thringsby." He seemed to feel that the matter was now settled.

"I'd intended to mention that, Stacey," Gordon said. "When we were alone. Mr. Orpington has been very generous. I was thinking of buying that Colonial Saltbox we were looking at a couple of months ago. The one you liked so much—out beyond Thringsby's Landing."

She remembered the place, but had it only been a couple of months ago? It seemed like another lifetime, another world. She shook her head, feeling slightly dazed.

"Oh, I know there were a few drawbacks about it." Gordon chose to misinterpret her gesture. "But there'll be enough left over to have those put right. Or we could look for another property. Perhaps bigger, with more land—"

The only real drawback to the place had been the idea of sharing it with Gordon. Stacey realized that now.

"Stacey, you would not marry this . . . this *parvenu*?" Hortense's hand crept into her own. "I will speak to Maman and Papa. They will introduce you to some suitable *messieùrs* in the *Diplomatique*—"

"My Mom and Dad," Marvin offered eagerly, "know lots of Army officers. Some of them will be Generals some day, like my Dad. They'll be glad to—"

"Marvin, shut up!" Alistair said. "You too, Hortense. If Stacey is having second thoughts—which wouldn't surprise me—*I'm* first in the queue."

"You?" Gordon looked at him with disdain. "What do *you* have to offer?"

"Not much," Alistair admitted, "at the moment. I

happen to believe I have an excellent career ahead of me. But I'll admit she'd be taking a chance—"

"Perhaps it's always a chance," Stacey said. "Even with someone you've known all your life. Or think you've known—"

"Life would be more fun with Al," Marvin voted loyally. "This guy's not only a crook, he's a stuffed shirt with it."

"Eustacia," Gordon said icily, "I don't see why we have to put up with all this. Can't you get rid of these brats?"

"I probably could, Gordon," she said. "If I wanted to. By the way, I prefer to be called Stacey. You've always done so. I don't know why you're suddenly calling me Eustacia." But she did. It was sheer snobbery. Gordon was trying to emulate Cousin Eustace, apparently not having noticed that he was not particularly endearing.

"It's your name—"

"And I don't like it. Please continue to call me Stacey—if you feel you must call me anything at all."

"Whatever you wish." Gordon gave the impression of shrugging, although, of course, he would never do anything so vulgar. "It's beside the point and I don't see why you bother to make an issue of it—"

"*I* do," Hortense said. "I have been thinking. I was born in April—why do I not use that for a name? It is prettier than Hortense."

"I think that's a very good idea," Stacey said warmly.

"April," Marvin said. "That's not bad. Ap, for short—"

"I will insist on the French way," Hortense said. "I will be called *Avril*."

"Avril? Av?" Marvin encountered her basilisk eye and surrendered. "Okay," he said. "Avril's fine with me."

"Stacey," Gordon said between clenched teeth. "I will *not* tell you again: get rid of these frightful brats!"

"You haven't the right to *tell* me anything!" Stacey flared. "And you're not going to have. Let *me* tell *you* something. Marvin's right. You're a stuffed shirt and a crook! Marry you? I never even want to *see* you again!"

Alistair led the applause. Eustace and Rowena did not join in.

"Unfortunately, I will have to see you one more time. I'm going to finish this job. I'm going to collect the Orphington Bequest after the Exhibition closes and return it personally to the museum—with no substitution along the way. And then you can have my resignation. But I'll leave a sealed letter for the Trustees to open if anything ever happens to the Bequest. So you'd better take good care to see that it isn't lost or stolen at any time in the future!"

"That's right," Alistair said. "To make sure, we'll drop in for a sentimental visit to it every now and again—after all, it brought us together."

"Yeah," Marvin said. "I'll look in too, and it better be there."

Gordon turned toward Marvin with a dangerous light in his eyes.

"I think that's all we have to say." Alistair moved in front of Marvin hastily. "We're leaving now, aren't we . . . Stacey?"

"Out into the clean fresh air," Stacey said dramatically, taking Hortense's hand.

The door slammed shut behind them.

"It was a great curtain line," Alistair said appreciatively. "I suppose, after that, we really couldn't have asked for the loan of Cousin Eustace's car to get us back to London?"

"We could *not!*"

"No, I hardly thought so," he said regretfully. "Pity. I've still got the keys..."

"He'd probably call the police," Marvin said. "Now that he hasn't got anything to lose."

"I'm afraid you're right again, Marvin." They turned into the main road and began plodding along.

"Now what do we do?" Marvin asked.

"I'm afraid we're stuck with you, Marvin, until your parents return next week. So I propose that we all catch the ferry to France and deliver Hortense to her aunts in Paris since her grandmother seems to be unavailable."

"Hey, great!" Marvin said. "I've never seen Paris."

"Neither have I." Stacey felt her spirits rising. This was going to be a holiday, after all.

"Then I can introduce Marvin to my family." Hortense accepted the decision philosophically; she had always known that this could not go on forever. She looked over her shoulder and forgot regrets.

"Here comes a green bus!" she cried. "It says London on the front—"

"And there's the bus stop ahead—" They broke into a shambling run, waving their arms wildly.

The driver smiled in sympathy as he opened the doors to the laughing family party.